Oaky With a Hint of Murder

Blue Dragon
Publishing

Oaky With a Hint of Murder
Published by Blue Dragon Publishing, LLC
Williamsburg, VA
www.BlueDragonPublishing.com
Copyright © 2024 by Dawn Brotherton

ISBN 978-1-939696-87-8 (paperback)
ISBN 978-1-939696-91-5 (ePub)

Library of Congress Control Number: 2023947349

Cover by Hakm Bin Ahmad

Printed in the U.S.A

28 27 26 25 24   1 2 3 4 5 6 7

Oaky With a Hint of Murder

DAWN BROTHERTON

Chapter 1

Aury St. Clair wrapped her hands around the mug and held the blueberry-flavored coffee under her nose to savor the smell. Wearing an oversized sweater and a pair of gray yoga pants, she tucked her legs under her and finally allowed herself to relax. The stone patio with its cushioned furniture was the perfect place to take in the flowing green hills sloping down to the wide, expansive lake on this beautiful fall morning. The reflection of the colorful leaves dappled the surface of the water. She was overwhelmed by her good fortune and reached over to give Scott's hand an affectionate squeeze, happy to be with him and his family.

She breathed out a happy sigh. "The view is simply gorgeous."

Joyce Hamilton, the wife of Scott's cousin Ethan, stood beside the open glass door that bridged the patio and the winery's tasting room. In her bright, flowery sundress, she looked a decade younger than her forty-five years. "Ethan and I didn't know anything about making wine or growing grapes, but when we saw this piece of property on the Finger Lakes five years ago, we knew we had to figure it out."

"Isn't it awfully cold in the winter?" Scott asked. "New York gets a lot of snow."

"We were used to Pennsylvania winters, and Seneca Lake isn't much worse. Besides, there's always things to do indoors." Ethan refilled his coffee mug from the carafe on the table.

The dark stubble on his face and his red flannel shirt reminded Aury of a lumberjack.

"I'm glad you were able to come during our fall break. That gives us a few days to visit uninterrupted. I'm happy to relinquish my professor duties to be a vintner's wife and tour guide." As a professor in the computer engineering college at Cornell University, Joyce was tied to the academic calendar.

"And just in time for the wine festival." Ethan lifted his mug in salute. "You're going to sample wines from all over the region without having to drive around the eleven major lakes."

"How many wineries are there in the Finger Lakes?" Aury asked.

"Easily over a hundred. Not to mention breweries and distilleries." Joyce crossed the room and sat at the table.

"We may have to stay longer." Scott squeezed Aury's hand.

"You'll get no complaints from me." She smiled into his pale blue eyes.

"Where's Liza this morning? I would have thought she would have been up by now," Ethan said.

Aury laughed. "Gran's long gone. She spotted a quilt store when we drove into town last night and was off bright and early this morning to see if they had any good deals."

"Oh, she'll like the ladies who run the Grape Basket Quilt Shop. They're quite the duo. I think they're the town's welcome wagon." Joyce took a muffin from the table and passed around the basket. "We hadn't even unpacked when they arrived at our door with goodies, and the basket was covered with an intricate picnic quilt. I couldn't stand to use it on the ground, so it's hanging in the tasting room."

Scott put a slice of pumpkin bread on the plate in front of Aury and selected a raspberry scone for himself. "We'll be lucky if we can fit the fabric Liza picks up in our car for the trip home." Scott grinned to soften his words.

"Leave some room for the wine," Ethan reminded him. "You said you'd serve some at Eastover."

"That takes priority. Don't tell Liza."

"Don't tell me what?" Gran strode onto the patio, her long skirt flowing behind her. The cloth band on her wide-brimmed hat matched the print on her homemade shopping bag.

"You're back! That was a fast shopping trip for you. What did you find?" Aury stood and slid a chair out for her grandmother to sit beside her. As she took in the striking white of Gran's curls, Aury tried to remember when she had passed her grandmother's height of five and a half feet. Aury had stopped growing some time ago, so perhaps age was shrinking her grandmother ever so slightly, but there was no diminishing the ferocious strength hidden by Gran's slight frame.

"I saw some things you'd like, so we'll need to go back." Before taking a seat, Liza helped herself to a cup of coffee and a scone. She nestled the bulging shopping bag at her feet. "Those quilt ladies can talk your ear off."

Scott and Aury exchanged a knowing smile as Aury took her seat again.

"I saw that." Liza added a sugar cube to her coffee and stirred. "What a joy they are! They seem to know everyone in this town. And a few towns over, come to think of it."

"Clara and Mable grew up here. They helped us settle in," Joyce said.

Liza lowered her voice conspiratorially and leaned in. "Well, if you need odd jobs done, don't hire Ricky Nelson. Seems he has the habit of over-promising and under-delivering." Liza bit into the pastry. "Hmmmm. I'm going to need this recipe."

"How do you do that?" Scott asked.

"Do what?" Liza licked sugar from her thumb.

"Get to know people so quickly. Give them ten minutes and you'll get their life story."

"It's a gift."

Aury chuckled at her grandmother's response, but Scott

was right. Gran could charm almost anyone. There was something about her honest interest that made people want to confide in her. Aury looked over the fields again. "I can't get over how beautiful it is here. We really needed a little time to relax."

"I was thinking this would be an exquisite place for a wedding," Joyce said, not so subtly, as she slipped her hand into her husband's, the dark brown of her skin a beautiful contrast to Ethan's pale arm.

"Don't pressure them. They haven't been engaged that long." Behind a theatrical hand, Ethan stage whispered to Aury, "But wait until you see the garden in full bloom. The pictures would be unbelievable."

The heat rose in Aury's neck and face as Scott draped his arm around her. "We haven't set a date yet. We just got Eastover turning a profit, thanks to Aury's accounting skills. I'd be lost without her. I'm sure we will get around to setting a date one of these days."

Aury was thankful for Scott's patience concerning the wedding. Although she had no doubt she wanted to spend the rest of her life with him, they needed to decide what form the wedding day would take. Her first wedding had been a lavish affair, so at thirty-nine, she didn't want a big ceremony this time. But this was Scott's first marriage, and he wanted to show her off. They were still negotiating the details.

"Eastover is an important investment. I'm thankful we were able to turn it into the kind of retreat center Scott's parents had wanted," Aury said.

When Scott had inherited the floundering property from his parents, the money for upkeep hadn't come with it. Aury's accounting skills had helped Scott turn things around. The time they spent working together had given their friendship time to blossom into something even more special.

"It feels like we've barely left the property since the storm that trapped Aury and her sewing sisters inside the manor house." Scott grinned at Aury. "Thankfully Alan is overseeing everything while we're gone so we could sneak in a vacation.

He worked for my father for years, and I trust him implicitly."

"It's great that you have someone to watch over things. When we left Songscape to visit you, I thought Ethan was going to have a panic attack. He must have called back to check on things a few times a day, and we were closed for the weekend!" Joyce laughed.

"I wasn't that bad," Ethan protested.

Joyce patted his hand. "If you say so, dear."

Scott laughed at Joyce's sarcastic tone. "Eastover is as much of a home to Alan as it is to us. It's in great hands, but I can't say that I'm not constantly thinking about what I'm missing or need to be doing."

"Getting married at Eastover would make so much sense, seeing as that's where you met." Liza removed her hat and balanced it on top of her packages.

"You promised to tell us about your ghost." Aury gracefully changed the topic before it centered on the wedding date again.

Joyce set down her cup and moved to the edge of her seat. "We had heard the story before we bought the place, of course—"

"From the quilters, as a matter of fact," Ethan added.

"Native Americans occupied this land thousands of years before European settlers showed up," Joyce said.

"Wasn't it the Iroquois?" Liza asked.

"They don't refer to themselves as Iroquois. That was a French insult meaning *black snake*," the professor corrected with a smile.

"They are the Haudenosaunee Confederacy, which is actually a collection of six nations: the Cayuga, Mohawk, Oneida, Onondaga, Seneca, and Tuscarora, who shared the fruits of the land without believing they owned anything." Ethan took a bite of his food and nodded to his wife for her to go on.

"Together, the Confederacy held off English colonization for a long time. It wasn't until the Revolution, when some of the nations supported the British and others the Americans, that the Haudenosaunee Confederacy had their own civil war and diminished in strength. Eventually, the Continental Army drove many of them from the Finger Lakes."

Joyce clearly knew her history and settled in for the story telling. "There are so many Native American legends from this area. They believed the Creator reached down and blessed this land, and the Finger Lakes are the fingerprints of the Creator. This is sacred ground to them. Thankfully, Haudenosaunee members have remained in this area all along."

Ethan wiped his hands on a napkin. "Did the rumbles disturb you last night?"

Aury nodded. "Now that you mention it, I heard the noise, but it didn't register. I lived near the Naval Weapons Station for years, so explosions don't phase me anymore. The military is constantly blowing things up or playing war games."

"Well, in the Native American Creation story, Sky Woman gave birth to twin sons: Flint and Sapling. Sapling created everything good, while Flint tried to destroy Sapling's work. Legend has it that the noise comes from the Thunder Beings who were appointed by the Creator to strike down the evil things that Flint made. So that would be the thunder heard over the earth and waters. Others claim evil spirits inhabit the lake," Joyce said.

"Don't forget the one about the Revolutionary War soldier who got lost and is trying to contact his regiment. Around here, they call it the Seneca Drums." Ethan raised his eyebrows skeptically and stood.

"So what is it really?" Liza asked.

Aury loved her grandmother. She was all about getting to the bottom of things.

"I'm not sure. But now folks are saying that Flint or the soldier is the one messing around in our vineyard," Joyce said. "I don't believe in ghosts, but something strange is going on."

Aury sat straight. Someone messing in the vineyard didn't sound like good news for the business. "What do you mean?" Now Aury was the one who wanted to get to the bottom of things.

"First, it was the lights flickering. It wasn't constant—maybe once a week and usually when the tasting room was full." Ethan shook his head. "I figured it was the wiring, but it had been inspected two months earlier. I called in the electrician, and she didn't find anything. Two weeks later, it started again. I checked with the neighbors, and no one else had the same problem. We complained to the power company. They weren't any help. Said they'd send someone out next time it happened, but by the time they showed up, the power was steady. It hasn't happened lately. I thought I was losing it."

"The jury's still out on that." Joyce reached up to swat Ethan's back as he stood by her side.

"We'd open the tasting room, and furniture would be different than how we left it. Megan, who started working with us shortly after we got here, almost quit over that. She gets spooked pretty easily and was convinced the place was haunted," Ethan said.

Aury mussed Scott's short hair, smiling at the slight streak of gray. "You two should get along great, such scaredy pants."

"Ha, ha," he said sarcastically. "I'll take drinking wine with a lost soldier over a graveyard in the dark woods of Eastover any day."

When Scott and Aury were searching the Eastover property for a hidden treasure, Scott confided that, when he was little, he was afraid to go into the fog-shrouded woods because he thought they were haunted.

She wrapped her arms around his neck. "I'll protect you from the mean old ghosts."

"You're making me sorry I told you that story from my childhood," he muttered good naturedly. "No one in their right mind would venture into haunted woods."

"That's what your grandparents were counting on when they spun that tale." Liza hooted with laughter.

"You probably won't get to drink with the ghost in the tasting room. Megan did a spiritual cleansing, and things stopped moving around." Joyce leaned forward to refill her coffee.

"Oh, right. That was it. It didn't have *anything* to do with the security cameras I installed." Ethan smirked at Joyce. "Although I really wish I could figure out how it happened."

Aury's curiosity was piqued. Someone was haunting this winery, but she didn't put any stock in the idea of the supernatural.

Joyce ignored her husband's expression. "Now the eerie cries in the night have joined the drums, and it's starting to scare off patrons. They don't want to be here after dark."

"That's particularly annoying because we spent all that money to put in the firepits and expand the patio so we could have live music out here in the evening." Ethan waved his arm to indicate the yard.

"What are you going to do?" Scott asked Ethan.

Aury stood. "I know what *we're* going to do. Let's catch ourselves a ghost."

Chapter 2

"Get back here!" The yell broke into their conversation. A black Labrador puppy with large paws scampered across the stone patio and slid under Scott's chair.

Scott reached down and pulled the pup into his lap, smiling as he cradled the dog. "Treasure, what kind of mischief have you been up to?"

Aury placed a hand on his shoulder and beamed at her fiancé who turned into a doting puppy owner. Although Scott had gifted her the puppy under the pretense to keep her company when she moved to Eastover, Aury recognized Treasure as equally Scott's companion.

A harried, gangly man in his mid-twenties rounded the corner, stopping short at seeing the group around the table. "I didn't mean to disturb you."

An Australian Shepherd with a beautiful coat mottled with blacks, browns, tans, and white trotted up behind the man and sat protectively beside Joyce. She stroked his head warmly. "Matthew, these are our guests, Scott, Aury, and Liza. They're visiting from Virginia."

Ethan added, "Matthew worked for the previous owner and agreed to stay on when we bought the winery. He does most of the maintenance around here and knows more about the vines than I do. He's been a blessing."

"I see you met Treasure. What did she do this time?" Aury asked Matthew.

"She and Elvis were digging out by the vines. They made quite a mess."

"Elvis was digging? That's curious," Joyce remarked.

"He's been sniffing around there a lot lately."

"If they were digging, they might have been chasing an animal. Could have been a mole." Ethan bent down to scratch behind Elvis's ears. "You were just protecting the fields, weren't you?"

"Did they hurt anything?" Scott asked.

"No, but I'll need to get a spade to fill in the holes." Matthew nervously tightened the tuck on his button-down linen shirt.

"Thanks for taking care of it. I was hoping to show our guests around town and maybe get in a quick hike near one of the waterfalls." Ethan stood back up and stretched. "Megan will take care of the lunch crowd, but she may need some help with the tastings. It's supposed to be a marvelous day, and that makes people thirsty."

"Not a problem. I'll get to it. Nice meeting you folks." Matthew didn't meet their eyes and quickly made for the work shed.

"Matthew and Megan have been a huge help keeping this place going," Ethan explained. "Megan's the young lady who conducts most of the tastings, although she barely seems old enough to drink. She grew up around here and spent her college summers working part-time at other wineries, so I was lucky to get her."

Joyce snickered a little. "Megan connects well with people, even with her constant talk about the supernatural and crystals."

Ethan grinned and shook his head. "Matthew's a little resistant to the small changes I've been trying to implement around here but usually comes around if I explain my reasoning to him. He's used to how the previous owner did things. I think it's just an adjustment for him."

"I'm sorry if Treasure's causing problems. She's still so

young, we didn't want to leave her in a kennel. Thankfully she's housebroken," she smiled at Scott, "and adores her doggie bed."

Scott's mouth twitched into a grin. "No way Aury would let her sleep in a human bed."

Aury shuddered at the thought. "And chance ruining a quilt? Not on your life."

"She's no problem at all," Ethan said. "This is a wonderful place for dogs to run, and Elvis won't let her get into any trouble. He's a good protector." At the sound of his name, the Aussie pushed his head under Ethan's hand.

"Elvis?"

Joyce laughed. "That's my fault. My dad taught me to dance to Elvis Presley. I love his music. When we picked out our colorful pup, the name just seemed to fit."

"Is the love of music where you got the name for the winery? Or was it the Songscape Winery when you bought it?" Scott asked.

"It was Dreamscape Winery, but we wanted to tweak the name a bit to make it special to us without losing the heritage of the previous owner." Ethan patted Elvis's head.

"We can't wait to see the rest of the place. The guestrooms are so comfortable and nicely furnished," said Liza.

"I had fun decorating them myself. People often assume because I'm into computers that I don't have a creative side. But trust me, you need to be awfully creative to code some of the tasks we're given at times." Joyce's broad smile was infectious.

Aury could easily picture this tall, imposing woman in front of a classroom, but as she watched Joyce mischievously pull at Elvis's tail, she wondered if professor let this side of her show in front of the students.

"I love how I have seen a music theme throughout so far. Is it in all the rooms?" Liza dabbed at her mouth with a napkin and placed it beside her empty plate.

"It was fun rummaging around in old barns on antiquing

weekends, foraging for unique items. I found the old trombone that's in your room, Liza, in someone's hayloft." Joyce's eyes twinkled at the memory.

"Well, you've done a wonderful job." Scott grabbed another scone from the near-empty plate. "Maybe we should hit some garage sales to furnish the older cabins at Eastover."

"I *am* looking for inexpensive ways to redecorate," Aury admitted. Fixing up the property came with a large price tag. She and Scott still had plans for improvements and more staff, so Aury kept a close watch on their budget. But she couldn't have been happier to trade in her office job to work alongside Scott.

Scott took her hand and shook it a little to break her reverie. "Don't get lost in your plans right now. Didn't you say we were going to catch a ghost? Where do you think we should start?"

"I think you need to get to know the town a little more," Joyce suggested. "That will help you understand why there's no way we're leaving, even if there is a ghost."

Chapter 3

It was shaping up to be a perfect day as the group ambled down Main Street. Aury had pulled her dark hair into a ponytail and traded her sweatshirt for a light sweater. She and Scott walked hand in hand behind Ethan and Joyce as they pointed out sights of interest to Liza. The last-century architecture was well maintained and painted in a variety of pastel colors.

As they passed the library, Liza wanted to take a quick peek inside.

"Gran, you can't use quick peek and library in the same sentence." Aury prodded her along. "You can come back later and spend as much time here as you want."

"Joyce, is it true there's a library on the Cornell campus that resembles Hogwarts?" Liza's eyes twinkled like a child's.

"Yep, and it's a beautiful library, but I don't think it's that similar to the movie set. If you want, we can visit later this week."

"I would love that, dear. Thank you." Liza smiled in appreciation. "Oh, here's that café the quilt ladies told me about. Let's stop for lunch." Liza turned to enter the restaurant without waiting for a response.

The bell chimed, announcing their arrival, and the group were immediately met by a young waitress holding menus. Ushered to a round table near the window, they sat to peruse the menu. Healthful salads full of fresh fruit offset the paninis

17

and creamy, rich soups. After they placed their orders, Joyce continued the tour verbally. "Once upon a time, this building was a soda fountain and apothecary."

Rather than a rundown appearance, the room's outdated wallpaper and dark trim made walking into the café feel like stepping back in time. The mismatched wooden chairs added character.

Joyce nodded to the glass cases. "See the bakery items over there? There used to be bar stools and a counter where you could get a root-beer float for a nickel."

"Ah, some of my best dates started with a root beer float." Liza stared dreamily at the non-existent bar stools.

"Do tell, Gran. Was Grandpa one of those best dates?" Aury smiled fondly.

Liza rested her hand on Aury's arm. "He was the best of the best. But that doesn't mean I didn't have a magnificent time exploring my options until he came along."

The group laughed when Liza wiggled her eyebrows. Aury's grandfather had died of cancer when Aury was young, but Gran never remarried. Liza always told her no one could compete with her Robert.

The food arrived, and as they ate, Scott filled Ethan and Joyce in on the plans for Eastover—what had been accomplished and what was still on the to-do list. Aury was toying with the idea of a cabin where visitors could try their hand at various arts and crafts.

"I'm not sure it's such a good idea," Scott admitted, giving Aury an apologetic look. "Once we get that set up, she may never want to come out. Then who's going to help me with the heavy lifting?"

Aury gave him a teasing nudge with her shoulder. "I'm sure Gran will help you, but I'll make sure to set up visiting hours in the craft cabin in case you want to see me."

Liza rolled her eyes and addressed Joyce. "I want to hear more about this town. I love history."

Joyce obliged. "The hardware store across the street has

been there since the 1800s. It used to be a feed and seed but now carries a little of everything. It takes up most of the block. The bookstore at the corner is one of my favorites. They have cozy chairs to sink into while you sample the latest titles. But I really love that they carry a lot of local authors. You'll find extensive books about the history of this area on their shelves."

Ethan highlighted the local boating museum and the tall steeple of the historic church. "Many abolitionists preached from the pulpit in that church."

"And, of course, there's the Grape Basket, which Liza already discovered," finished Joyce. "Everyone here has been so warm and inviting."

"Not quite everyone," Ethan mumbled.

Joyce elbowed him, but no further explanation was offered.

Aury liked this little town. It felt much older than Williamsburg, Virginia, and held quite a bit of charm. Unlike the New Town area of Williamsburg with its modern stores and restaurants, this village could have easily been from the last century. She hadn't seen any chain stores or fast-food restaurants. It was as if they had traveled back in time.

After the lure of the café, Aury half-expected to see horses and buggies on the street when they walked outside.

A young man in his early twenties bumped into Joyce as the group paused to decide where to go next. He glanced up from his phone long enough to apologize. "I'm sorry, Mrs. Hampton. I shouldn't be texting and walking. Mom's always getting on me about that."

"It's all right, Kevin." Joyce placed her hand on his arm as he tucked the phone into his back pocket. "Meet our cousins who have come for a visit."

Joyce made the introductions warmly, and Aury again silently thanked God for allowing her to be a part of this family.

"I've always wanted to see Williamsburg. We went there on vacation when I was little, but I don't remember it. I've seen the pictures enough times though." Kevin laughed and shook his head. "Mom loves a good scrapbook and telling stories."

"That's what moms are supposed to do. You'll appreciate it someday." Liza's eyes twinkled.

"Well, I better get going. I have food deliveries to make. Nice meeting you." Kevin waved as he dipped into the store. He pulled out his phone again before the door had time to close.

"Kevin's a hard worker. I would never say it in front of his mother, but it would be good for him to get out of this area to find a job." Joyce watched him through the café's window. "He works a number of part-time jobs, but I think he could do better for himself."

"His mother doesn't want him to leave?" Aury asked.

Ethan shook his head. "That woman holds onto him so tightly, I'm surprised he can breathe."

Joyce lowered her voice. "From what I hear, she had a rough time getting pregnant, and Kevin's an only child. He's got allergies and sensitivities, so she's constantly watching over him."

"You ask me, she needs to let him grow up. Half his *sensitivities* are probably brought on by his mother's anxiety," Ethan scoffed.

Joyce sighed and herded the group down the tree-lined street. Aury admired the quaintness of the stores they passed.

Scott clapped his hands together. "While you ladies rake through the quilt store, Ethan's going to take me to the furniture store. They have a handmade selection I want to check out. We'll meet up with you in an hour."

"Better make that two," Liza said, picking up her step.

Scott raised his eyebrows at her. "Didn't you buy fabric this morning?"

She stopped, putting her hands on her hips. "Your point?"

Laughing, Scott turned and kissed Aury's cheek. "Text me when you're ready to go."

The men turned left while the ladies went right.

Joyce guided them to the town's quilt store. "The Finger Lakes Region has such a rich history, and many famous people lived here or came here to escape the summer heat—folks like Harriet Tubman, Frederick Douglas, Susan B. Anthony, Mark Twain, and so many more, I can't name them all." Joyce threw up her hands. "And the buildings; don't even get me started! The Trinity Episcopal Church is simply gorgeous. You should visit it while you're here. It's made of stone with gothic and Romanesque features. I just love the stained glass."

"Churches are my second favorite things to old libraries." Liza opened the door to the Grape Basket.

"What about quilt stores?" Aury asked.

"They're in a league of their own." The women all laughed.

"Liza, back so soon?" The woman behind the counter wore a nametag that read "Mabel" in a bold, colorful font. Her wire-rimmed glasses hung from a beaded chain around her neck.

Clara waved her scissors from the cutting table where she was lining up fabric. The women were cut from the same cloth, both slightly taller than Liza, with gray hair, permed into tight curls, and styled short. Clara's thick-rimmed, rose glasses perched on the end of her nose.

"Yes, I brought my family." Liza introduced Aury then nodded toward Joyce. "You've met our cousin, I believe."

Aury loved how Gran so easily adopted Ethan and Joyce as cousins, although she and Scott weren't even married yet.

With a slight dip of the chin, they smiled at each other.

"We tried out the café you recommended. It was lovely, as you promised." Gran took off her hat and tucked it into her now-empty shopping bag before fluffing her hair a bit.

"Glad you liked it. Well, nothing new has come in since this morning," Mabel said.

"I wanted to show my granddaughter a fabric line I think she'll love. Don't worry about us." Liza steered Aury and Joyce to a display in the middle of the shop.

"Oh, I like those purples." Joyce pointed to the fabric on the far wall. "I'll be back there looking for material to make curtains."

Aury touched the soft cottons and admired the bright

21

patterns on the table. As she and Liza lined up bolts next to each other to test how they would complement each other, the door chimed. Three ladies in their mid-forties chatted like schoolgirls as they entered. They acknowledged Mabel with a wave and beelined for the new-arrivals section two tables over from Liza and Aury.

Their random prattle was background noise as Aury tried to decide between the green or the blue tone for the bed quilts she was designing, which would be used in the retreat center's guest rooms.

"Is that Joyce Hampton from the Songscape Winery?"

Aury's ears perked up, and she touched Gran. Giving a tip of her head, Aury focused Gran's attention on the ladies' conversation.

"I think you're right," the slightly overweight woman with pasty skin said. "I hear they're having trouble. Something about the electricity not being stable."

"That's not a good thing for a business," the woman with brown, curly hair said.

Aury snuck a peek in her direction. The woman was overdressed for a shopping trip, wearing heels and a full face of makeup as if ready for a night on the town.

The curvaceous women with a short Afro said, "It's probably the Haudenosaunee Chief searching for his buried treasure."

The three women laughed.

"Are you going to the paint-and-sip party at Flo's studio? I hear Songscape Winery is providing the wine. I'm looking forward to trying it." The pasty-skinned woman held a bolt of fabric up to the light.

The heeled woman scoffed. "Ethan Hampton's a beginner. Don't expect much."

"Chantel, why aren't you catering the wine?" the woman with the Afro asked. The loud colors and bold patterns she perused matched the style of her wide-legged pants.

Now Aury had a name to match with the heeled woman.

"Flo felt she needed to give the newbies a chance. Apparently Hampton wowed her during a private tasting he gave her."

"How private?" the pale woman said with a snicker.

The implication made Aury bristle. Gran rested her hand on Aury's arm to keep her from saying anything.

"Ruthanne, don't be starting rumors. Flo doesn't deserve that." She wrapped a length of fabric around her waist. "Wouldn't this make a fabulous skirt?"

"Naomi, you have a pair of pants with similar colors. Why don't you branch out more? Try this." Chantel pushed a solid, light green bolt into her hands.

Naomi peered at it with disgust. "Have you seen my skin tone? This is not my style."

The women went on debating the best colors to compliment Naomi's figure, while Aury and Liza took their selections to the cutting table.

Liza cozied up to Clara conspiratorially. "What's this paint party they're talking about?"

"You should totally go! Everyone's invited. Flo has a wonderful art studio at the end of Main Street—the Cluster. She's opening it up for people to come in and try their hand at painting. She provides all the supplies, and it's catered."

"I'm not much of a painter, but my granddaughter is extremely crafty," Liza said.

Clara waved her scissor hand in dismissal. "You don't have to paint. Some people only go for the food and wine. Songscape Winery is supplying the drinks this year."

"Did I hear you mention our winery?" Joyce joined them at the cutting table, arms full of bolts in various shades of purple, violet, and magenta.

"I was saying they should go to the paint and sip at Flo's studio Monday night. It will be great fun." Clara folded the cut fabric. "Are you going?"

"Ethan and I are attending an event at the college that night. But, Aury, you all should go. Flo is a wonderful artist."

"We have tickets for sale here. Ask Mabel for them when you check out." Clara handed a stack of cut fabric and a sales slip to Aury and took Joyce's bundle.

"Scott's going to kill you if I get hooked on another hobby," Aury said to Gran.

"He'll have to catch me first!"

Chapter 4

1766 Genessee

"Kaintwakon, what are you doing on the water? You're supposed to be hunting." His mother carried a basket woven from the black ash tree and filled with clay pots and stirring utensils.

"I am protecting our village like a warrior," the eight-year-old *Onandowaga* boy declared from his perch on a fallen log resting in the water.

"You will be a hungry warrior if you don't go hunting."

He mumbled under his breath, picking up his bow and sliding the fallen arrows back into the quiver.

Genessee grinned as her son stomped away into the forest. *He is so much like his father,* she thought.

When they were growing up, her family had set up camp next to Hasanoanda's family. They played together frequently until his uncle took Hasanoanda under his wing to teach him about hunting and fishing. Hasanoanda also took his turn acting as a warrior, following large animals into new territories. They enacted hauling huge fish from the lake that would feed the village for weeks.

One of the most popular games was to stay afloat on a bobbing log, supposedly being tossed about by the whale-size fish. The boys in the nation competed to see who could stand on the log for the longest amount of time.

Genessee had applauded Hasanoanda's performance but also cleaned his wounds when he fell from a precarious tree branch or tumbled in the rocky creek banks.

It was fitting, so many years later, that their son would be acting out the same desire to be essential to the nation. She tended to his injuries in the same way, but he was a little harder to keep on task. When she was young, her parents would not have had to remind her about her duties. With the coming of the White men, larger game was more difficult to find. Her husband and the others had to travel farther to bring home meat for their village.

Genessee carried her basket to the water's edge. She was thankful for the warm stone to sit upon and the movement of the water that made the rinsing of cooking pots much easier. Her husband's trading with the French settlers had some value. In exchange for beaver furs, the Nation now had tools that were much stronger and lasted longer than what they were used to. They also gained blankets of a lighter weight than animal furs, which was a nice transition in the spring and fall.

But Genessee had doubts about their dealings. Already she witnessed changes in the younger warriors as they tried to imitate the ways of the White man. They spent less time listening to the old stories around the fire and more time spying on the camps where the French lived.

In no time, Kaintwakon broke through the trees, clutching a large hare by its hind legs. Blood dripped from his hand as he held up his prize.

"Well done, Little Warrior. Did you give thanks to the Great Creator?"

"Of course, Mother. This is not my first kill."

"Take it to the circle. Would you like my help skinning and preparing the meat?"

"I can do it myself." He started toward the village, calling over his shoulder, "But you can watch as I work if you would like."

Smiling, Genessee finished rinsing the articles in the lapping water. In no time, Kaintwakon would be spending more time away from the village. She wanted to watch over him while she could.

Chapter 5

Present day

The next morning, mist hung in the air like specters. Aury joined Ethan and Scott as they donned raincoats for a stroll around the vineyard while Liza and Joyce drove to Cornell to visit the Uris Library.

"I said I'd put you to work if you came in the fall. There are still more grapes to be harvested." Ethan stopped to examine the fruit hanging heavy on the vine. "We've finished the fields of Chardonnay, but I want to wait on the Cabernet Franc. The key is to pick them at their peak sugar."

Ethan lifted a bunch in his hand without taking it from the vine. "The longer the grapes stay on the vine, the more sugar they produce."

Aury regarded the fruit and marveled at the variety and complexity of growing grapes that she always took for granted. Seeing the rows and rows of vines attached to frames made from lines of wire reminded her of the grapevine quilt Gran had made for her parents when they got married. The purples and greens displayed intricate patterns that were only recognizable when studied closely.

She felt that way about the vines blooming in front of her now. From a distance, a green field spread before her. As she got closer, the rows were evident. Closer still and the bunches of ripening fruit punctuated the large leaves.

"When I think of wine country, I think of Napa Valley in California, not New York," admitted Scott.

Ethan nodded. "Grape growing is said to have started here when Reverend William Bostwick planted Catawba and Isabella grapes in the Hammondsport rectory garden in 1829. He freely gave out cuttings of his vines and encouraged others to plant them." They walked on until Ethan stopped to inspect the base of another plant.

"Instead of letting excess grapes rot, the Pleasant Valley Wine Company, also in Hammondsport, was established. They still use some of the original buildings and cellars carved into the hillside. It's worth checking out."

"Wait a minute. The temperance movement was in the early 1800s. How did a preacher get away with growing grapes for wine?" Scott asked.

"Bostwick and his fellow clergyman Deacon Samuel Warren marketed the wine mainly to churches for Holy Communion and to pharmacies for medicinal purposes. Gotta love their marketing strategy." Ethan pointed to the next field. "Let's go that way. I want to see where the dogs were digging."

As they walked, Ethan continued the history lesson. "A Ukrainian immigrant, Dr. Konstantin Frank, is credited with grafting European grape varieties with local grapes so we can now grow Rieslings, Gewurztraminer, Chardonnay, Pinot Noir, Merlot, Pinot Gris, and Cabernet Franc in this area. There are others too, of course."

"Do you grow all those grapes?" Aury let her fingers brush the grape leaves as they marched along. The serrated edges appeared as if they would be sharp but were soft and smooth.

Ethan shook his head. "No, I focus on Riesling, Chardonnay, Catawba, and Cabernet Franc. Ah, here's the spot Matthew mentioned."

Scott squatted to examine the ground. He pointed out raised patterns in the dirt. "These could be mole tunnels."

They followed the linear mounds as they ran alongside the vines.

"These vines aren't looking so good." Ethan analyzed

them closely. "See the withering leaves and the tiny buds? They should be much further along by now."

"Maybe it's the ghost." Aury was teasing, but Ethan's brow furrowed. Perhaps he was more worried about the strange happenings than he let on. She would have to get to the bottom of this so-called haunting before their vacation was over.

She took a different tack. "Could the animals be causing it?"

"I wouldn't think so. The—" Ethan's words were cut off.

"What do you think you're doing over there?" The gruff voice sounded from a grisly man in his late sixties. Thin and wiry, he needed suspenders to keep his tattered, faded, blue jeans from dragging when he walked through the field toward them.

"Mr. Reese, what can I do for you?" Ethan's tight smile didn't fool Aury. Reese's visit was not a pleasant one.

"Whatcha messing with? Can't you see them vines is dying off?"

"I was just pointing that out to my cousins. Aury, Scott, this is my neighbor Rodney Reese."

Aury and Scott didn't get a word out.

"Unless theys farmers, what good is telling 'em? Looks to me like you got a critter infestation." Reese stomped on a dirt mound, collapsing the tunnel underneath.

"I agree, but I don't see why that would be changing the plants like this." Ethan indicated the color of the leaves, shriveled and dark around the edges.

"That there looks like a soil problem." Reese harrumphed as he took in the other plants around him.

"What do you think is wrong with the soil?" Deep creases formed on Ethan's brow.

"You probably done messed it up with your new-fangled farming practices. We never had this problem when my daddy farmed this field."

Ethan's face flushed, but he retained his composure. "Mr.

Reese, your family hasn't owned this property for decades. A lot has changed since then."

"Better sample it and get 'er fixed before your problem becomes my problem." Reese pushed a filthy John Deere baseball cap to the back of his head.

"I guess I can do that. I'll have to find a lab. Maybe Cornell will test it for me."

"You don't need them snobby know-it-alls. My guy's just as good and ten times as quick, I'd wager."

"Okay." Ethan was hesitant. "I can get Matthew to drill a bore sample this afternoon."

"Have him bring it by my place." Reese turned, mumbling as he departed. "If you can't take care of what's ya got, it should come back to me where it rightly belongs."

The three watched him go until he passed the boundary markers outlining Ethan's property.

"What was that all about?" Scott asked.

Ethan picked a dying leaf off a plant, shredding it between his fingers as he talked. "The old man is still bitter from when his father sold the farm to my predecessor over thirty years ago. Reese senior was losing money and didn't have the cash to keep things going. He had to either sell part of his land or lose it all. He sold the grape fields and the winery and kept the orchards."

Aury shook her head. "Why is Reese taking it out on you? You didn't take his father's land."

"He tried to buy the land back when it went up for sale, but I don't think he was able to outbid me. Besides, I suspect the guy who owned this winery before didn't want to sell it to Reese anyway." Ethan tossed the leaf parts on the ground and wiped his hands together. "Let's head to the wine cellar. I'll show you the production end of winemaking."

They enjoyed their walk back. Although the fall air was crisp, the green leaves on the grape vines were barely showing signs of turning yellow. Aury imagined how magnificent the vineyard looked decked out in autumn colors. Somewhere in the distance, heavy machinery rumbled.

Aury attempted to pinpoint the source.

Ethan noticed her scanning the fields. "That tractor may be miles away. Sounds carry over the lake. It was really disturbing when we first moved here. I swear I jumped at every little noise until I got used to it."

"Hearing the frogs and insects all night long unnerved me when I first moved to Eastover. Now I don't even notice them." Scott picked up a fallen leaf larger than his hand.

"Coming from northern Virginia, you were probably used to the din of traffic lulling you to sleep." Aury put her arm around Scott.

The men discussed grape growing in Virginia versus New York. Aury mostly listened, having trouble shaking the unease from their encounter with Mr. Reese. Having such an unfriendly neighbor had to be uncomfortable for Joyce and Ethan. They were a very gracious and outgoing couple. Maybe he was the unwelcoming one Ethan had referenced yesterday.

The winery was built from thick, Eastern white pine logs with windows reaching to the roof's forty-foot peak. From the front, it resembled a European chalet, albeit a large one. A round river stone chimney split the front-facing windows up the middle. Colorful rocking chairs creaked gently in the breeze on the open front porch. Cheery windchimes jangled bright notes, but on this damp morning, no one lingered for the view.

As beautiful as the building was from the front, the interior far surpassed expectations. The tasting room held multiple solid, dark-timber countertops for patrons to sidle up to for a wine sample. Or guests could take a glass or wine flight to the heavy oak tables scattered throughout the open space. Couches and cushy loveseats faced the stone hearth. A box with music-themed trivia cards sat open on the coffee table in front of the seats. Above the mantle, a large painting showcased the Songscape logo backed by glorious purples, greens, and oranges. Not typically a color combination Aury would have thought to put together, but it fit this room beautifully.

Megan stood behind the bar, pouring and describing the wines to an older couple who were seated in front of her. She certainly looked like a pro, allocating just enough for a taste, then spinning the bottle as she lifted it from the glass to avoid any drips. Soft music emanated from hidden speakers.

Golden-amber pine planks covered the high ceilings in the tasting room. An open staircase led to more seating on the second floor. Tables and chairs were positioned next to the floor-to-ceiling windows facing the front lawn and rows of grapevines. Three of those tables were currently occupied with small groups, each sipping from glasses with liquids of various shades.

A second set of stairs in the back of the tasting room extended to the five guest suites, each with their own bathroom and small sitting area. This week, Aury, Scott, and Liza were enjoying the lodgings, courtesy of Ethan and Joyce. A sixth smaller room that Megan rented was on the first floor, down a hallway behind the tasting room.

"You've seen the glamorous parts of a winery. Now let me show you where all the work gets done." Ethan escorted them behind the largest bar, where they entered a hallway, passing offices and storerooms. At the end, he opened a double door that led to a landing overlooking a cavernous space.

As they followed him down two flights of lighted, metal stairs, the temperature dropped considerably. Aury shivered.

"This part is built into the side of the hill. It allows for a more consistent climate throughout the seasons." Ethan flipped a row of switches, replacing the dim illumination of the room with bright light. Despite the impression of being in a basement, the area was spotless with a white-tiled floor. Four silver vats shone brilliantly, each standing twenty feet tall with a ten-foot diameter, reminding Aury of small water towers.

Ethan ushered them through another set of double doors off to the right.

"When making white wine, grapes go into the bladder press as soon as we pick them." He patted a set of large doors on well-oiled tracks at the far end of the room. A heavy padlock clasped the ends of a thick chain together, holding the doors secure. "These barn doors roll open, and the truck backs right up to the press. The grapes get crushed, and various levels of filtration separate the stems and skins from the juice. Then we transfer the juice to the stainless-steel tanks we passed in the other room. In the tanks, the juice will ferment using the natural sugars."

"How long does that take?" asked Scott.

"Ten to twenty days. There are many factors we check along the way. We might add yeast if necessary. We can also adjust the temperature in the tanks to determine a sweet versus dry wine. I won't bore you with the details."

Aury poked Scott. "Now Scott's going to want to grow grapes. That's an awful lot of science."

He put his arm around her waist. "We can eat grapes without turning them into wine, you know."

Ethan smiled and continued moving toward another machine. "We've already sent the green grapes from the first two fields through the crush pad and de-stemmer. It's fermenting in stainless steel now." Ethan pointed to another press. "For red wines, we crush the grapes but let the skins and seeds soak in the juice for fifteen to thirty days in the fermentation tanks, depending on what we're going for. A lot of the flavor comes from the skin, along with the color. We also add yeast for the red wines." He gestured with an arm wave. "Let's go back into the fermenting room."

Scott and Aury followed Ethan. This time, Aury noticed the racks of wooden barrels that lined the wall under the stairs. "Is that for red wine?"

"Good guess. The juice in the fermentation tanks is pumped from the bottom of the tank and dumped into the top a few times a day to make sure there's even fermentation. Then the red wine goes into oak barrels for aging."

"Does aging mean months or years?" Aury asked.

"For our wines, only months to a year. Some vintners specialize and keep certain yields longer."

"How did you learn all this? I thought you were an insurance salesman." Scott's voice held a note of awe.

"Like you, I wasn't that excited about my previous profession. When Joyce came out to Cornell to interview for the job as a professor, we looked at property. I found out I could take classes for free, and Cornell is one of six places you can get a degree in viticulture. I don't think I'll go for the degree, but taking the classes I'm interested in has been extremely helpful."

"Still, that's a big leap. I wouldn't know where to start." Aury's eyes tried to take in the complex simplicity of it all. At first glance, the vats and barrels gave the impression of being very old-school, items read about in a historical Italian novel. But upon closer inspection, the gadgets reading temperature, humidity, air pressure, and other things Aury couldn't guess at were discretely placed throughout the room. Those were definitely part of the new age of winemaking.

"I started taking online classes right away. Then we moved up here the summer before Joyce started teaching, and the previous vintner gave me a crash course. It's been helpful to have Matthew around for continuity, and of course, Megan's an expert in the tasting room. She's from this area and took wine classes from Cornell as well." Ethan folded his arms and leaned against one of the racks. "I feel at home here."

"That's how I felt when I got out of the office and started working full time at Eastover. Maybe it's in our blood." Scott caressed the curve of the keg.

Aury looked at him lovingly and slipped her hand into his. "I see grapes in our future."

Not that she could blame him. It was a romantic notion. She pictured the layout of Eastover, considering the best location for a small vineyard. The property was situated on the bank of the James River, so she supposed water wouldn't be a problem.

"The bottling room is this way." Ethan exited through doors opposite the pressing room.

The young farmhand dressed in a light-blue linen shirt jumped when the trio entered.

"Matthew, good. I'm glad we ran into you. Will you please take a bore sample from that area where you found the dogs digging and drop it by Mr. Reese's farm? He's going to run some tests for me," Ethan said.

"Tests? What kind of tests? We have the pH sampler here." Matthew straightened his shirt.

"Some of the vines in that area don't look too great. He offered to help me get to the bottom of it."

Matthew tilted his head back and squinted. "Mr. Reese wants to help?"

Ethan chuckled. "I know. Doesn't sound right to me either. Just run the sample over there please. He's expecting it by the end of the day."

"Yes, sir. I gotta collect samples from the Cabernet Franc fields anyway. I'll do it right after I'm finished."

"That'll work."

Matthew took the clipboard he was writing on and slipped out a side door.

"Winemaking sure takes a lot of equipment," Scott said.

"It does, but we don't actually own a bottling machine. A mobile bottling company makes its way around to various wineries in the area. They pull their machine up to those barndoors, do their magic, and leave us with racks of bottled wine waiting to be labeled."

Aury groaned. "Please tell me you have a machine for that. I can't imagine doing it by hand."

"Sorry to hear you say that, because I was going to give you that opportunity." Ethan laughed at the dread on Aury's face. "Not all of it by yourself. I have students come in to help, and they earn a little spending money. We have quite a few colleges to pull from around here."

"Cornell and Ithaca. What else?" asked Scott.

"Finger Lakes Community College, Hobart and William Smith, Tompkins Cortland Community College. There are a few more but I don't remember all of them." Ethan indicated a rack of bottled wine. "If the Chardonnay is ready before you leave, you might get the chance to label some of the bottles you take back with you."

"That's kind of cool," she admitted.

"Don't worry, we have a process that makes it go smoothly once you get into the rhythm of it."

They exited through the same door Matthew had used. The ground sloped up a paved driveway to the side of the winery and a gravel parking lot. Because the winery had been built into the side of a hill, one side of the driveway paralleled the rear of the building. A stone wall held back the grassy slope on the other side.

"All this talk about work has made me hungry." Scott rubbed his hands together.

Ethan placed a hand on Scott's shoulder. "We offer a full food menu to complement the wine. Let's grab lunch. Joyce and Liza should be back by now."

"Not if Gran got lost in the stacks." Aury grinned from ear to ear.

As the group hiked back to the tasting room, Aury felt her smile fade. She knew it was her overdeveloped affinity for trouble—as Scott called it—but something was amiss in the hills of Seneca Lake. Someone or something was troubling Ethan. Sunshine and green vines couldn't hide the truth. There was something in the air, and it wasn't the fresh grapes.

Chapter 6

Elvis patiently endured Treasure's trounces and miniature snarls as the pup circled him. Occasionally a quick cuff from the Aussie knocked the Labrador off her oversized feet. The grassy area behind the tasting room and barn made for a perfect playground.

"Will you look at how well they get along? You'd think they were related," said Liza.

"Families come in all forms." Aury thought about how easily Scott and Ethan accepted their roles as cousins, although they had only recently discovered each other. If it hadn't been for Liza's genealogy search, Scott would have missed out on this branch of his family tree. And Joyce had immediately welcomed Aury, even though their connection wasn't official yet. "I wonder how the men are doing."

"What are they working on this afternoon?"

"They're setting up the stage for tonight's band. Ethan needed help getting the lighting right."

A movement from the wine cellar doorway caught their attention. Gran placed a hand above her brow to shield her eyes from the sun. "Who's that old man? He doesn't work here, does he?"

Aury stood and brushed herself off. "That's the neighbor I told you about—Reese. Let me see what he needs."

She left Liza to watch the dogs and strolled casually to the cellar. "Is there something I can help you with, Mr. Reese?"

Reese flinched at her voice. Then, squinting his eyes against the sunlight, he pulled himself to his full height of just under six feet. "Why are you skulking around back here?"

She inwardly groaned at his attempt to turn the tables on her. "That's what I should be asking you, Mr. Reese. I'm staying here. What's your excuse?"

It took Reese a moment to come up with a response. Aury waited impassively, arms crossed in front of her.

"Where's Ethan? I got the test results like I said I would," he said gruffly.

Treasure charged toward Aury, barking as furiously as a young pup can. She scooped her up, quieting her yaps.

"He and Scott are working on the patio for tonight's entertainment."

"That God-awful music again? Tell him he better keep it down. I'm not shy about calling the sheriff."

I'm sure you're not, she thought. "They finish by nine-thirty, so it won't interrupt your beauty sleep."

Reese bristled. "Don't get sassy with me, girl."

It was Aury's turn to fume, but she stayed on the high ground. "Mr. Reese, why don't you give me the test results, and I'll make sure Ethan gets them? I'm sure you're too busy to hang around here."

He harumphed. "The tests were negative for anything out of the ordinary. Them vines are probably dying because he doesn't have the sense God gave him to trim them right."

Aury swallowed her retort. "I'll pass along the message. Have a good day." She turned her back on him. Treasure barked at Reese over her shoulder.

When Aury reached Liza, she released Treasure, who immediately pounced on Elvis. He took it in stride, rolling Treasure over and placing a paw on her chest to hold her in place.

"What was that all about?" Liza asked.

"That old curmudgeon was here to see Ethan."

"Why was he in the cellar? Couldn't he hear the noise

they're making out back? Or see them if he went through the tasting room?"

Aury shrugged. "He's not much of a conversationalist." Treasure bounded up to her, and she crouched to scratch behind the dog's ears.

"Let's go check on the progress. Help me up, would you, dear?" Liza extended her hand, and Aury gave her support to pull herself up.

Aury's diamond engagement ring caught the sun and sparkled. The thought of the hidden treasure she and Scott had uncovered brought a smile to her lips. This beautiful ring was not only a symbol of their love, but also of their adventures together—in the past and those yet to come.

As she and Liza traipsed up the slope to the front of the winery, tires on an old Ford pickup truck spun, kicking up gravel. Aury instinctively threw a hand up to cover her head as she turned her face away. Liza did the same thing, but Elvis bounded after the truck, barking his disapproval.

"Now if he isn't an immature fella, I don't know who is," Liza said. "Why doesn't that man act his age?"

Aury shook her head sadly. "Mr. Reese doesn't seem to have much respect for anything that isn't his." *Or anything he thinks should be,* she thought.

White lights twinkled from the strands zigzagging above the patio and down to the stage. The sun was setting, leaving a slight chill in the air. As Aury grabbed a sweater from her room, the opening notes from the band's first set drifted up the stairs. She hurried to join the others.

Scott motioned her into the seat next to him and slid his arm around her shoulders.

Aury looked around appreciatively. "This is a nice turn out. I thought Ethan was worried about it."

"This band is really popular with the older college crowd. I guess they decided to brave the ghosts." Joyce poured them a round of wine.

Scott took a sip. "This wine is worth braving a league of ghosts!"

"I'm glad you like it. It's one of my favorites. We bottled it our first season here. We named it *Love Me Tender* and save it for special guests."

"An Elvis Presley song! Good choice." Liza raised her glass in a toast.

Joyce handed Aury a wine list from the table. "Look over our selection. You may want to try a flight so you can sample them all."

Aury read aloud. *"You May Be Right."*

"Billy Joel." Joyce gave the description, "With this Chardonnay, you can taste lemongrass and nuts. Because it's oaked in neutral French barrels, there isn't a woody flavor, but it's very smooth."

Aury read the next one on the list. *"If I Can Dream."*

"Oh, I love that Elvis song." Liza swayed to the music in her head.

"That's a blend of Catawba and Cab Franc. It's a bit peppery with the taste of plum on the backend," Joyce said.

"How do you keep all these straight?" Liza asked.

Joyce laughed. "We tasted a lot of wines to get here, trust me. But for the wines Ethan makes, I've explained them to clients so many times, it's rote memory."

Aury picked up the list again. *"Look What You Made Me Do* by Taylor Swift, *Come Together* by the Beatles, *Under Pressure* by Queen."

Joyce looked delighted. "That's our sparkling wine. Ethan came up with that name, and he's quite proud of it."

A couple timidly approached the circle of lights. Joyce stood. "Excuse me. I still need to work for a little longer tonight. Megan is busy pouring tastings, and Ethan is chatting with people inside." She glided through the crowd to escort the couple to an empty table.

Aury snuggled into Scott. "I could get used to this."

He kissed the top of her head. "What about you, Liza? Ready to move to New York?"

"No way. I'm a southern girl. I'd freeze to death up here in the winter." She held up her wine. "Doesn't mean a few weeks here in the summer wouldn't be good for me."

They clinked glasses.

When the band finished its second set, the crowd began to thin. Aury noticed many went into the shop to get bottles to take home before they left. That was a good sign.

She took advantage of the break to go inside for water. While she was filling a pitcher for the table, she overheard Ethan talking with some customers. They acted upset, and he was apologizing profusely.

"I will of course pay to have your tire repaired." He caught Aury's eye. "Can you see if Scott can give me a hand changing a tire?"

"Sure." Aury carried the water to the table. "Scott, Ethan needs your help. A customer has a flat tire."

Scott jumped up. "Save my seat."

Liza raised an eyebrow. "Doesn't Ethan know how to change a tire?"

"He's juggling a lot of things. Having Scott help gives him one less thing to worry about."

The band started their final set. After four songs, Joyce rushed by. Aury caught her wrist. "What can I do?"

Joyce gave a tight smile. "Nothing really. I appreciate it, but I think the guys have it handled." She hurried away.

"How long does it take them to change a tire?" Liza wondered out loud.

Liza and Aury listened to the music and doodled new quilt pattern ideas on napkins while they waited for the others to return. Liza had been inspired by the greens and purples of the fields and had purchased fabric from the Grape Basket that captured that essence.

"The yellow the guild used in Scott's Eastover quilt would

make a great accent color here." Aury pointed to triangles along the border.

"Wonderful idea." Liza wrote a note on the napkin and slipped it into her pocket, so the design didn't get swept away with the trash.

Aury glanced at her watch. The band was finishing their last number, and Scott still hadn't returned. Megan was clearing dishes from empty tables.

"Gran, let's go see what's happening." They made their way through the nearly empty tasting room and out the front door.

Scott was waving a flashlight, directing traffic in the parking lot. Ethan signaled a path around a set of orange cones in the center of the lot.

Liza and Aury watched until no cars were moving before they ventured onto the gravel. "What's going on?" Aury asked.

Ethan produced pieces of metal from his pocket. "Nails! Can you believe it? Someone dumped nails in the parking lot!"

"Punctured a few tires." Scott clicked off his flashlight. "Sorry. I didn't mean to desert you."

"No worries." Aury gave him a quick hug. She turned to Ethan. "Who would dump nails? It had to be an accident, right?"

"Or that old fool and his pickup," Gran muttered.

"What old fool?" Ethan asked.

"When Mr. Reese was here earlier, he left in quite a hurry," Aury explained.

"The way he took off outta here, trash could have easily fallen from his truck bed."

"I guess that could have happened, but it was more than just one or two. We changed three tires before we traced the source of the problem." Ethan was fit to be tied. "I better go help Joyce."

"We'll all help clean up. Don't you worry." Liza patted him on the back. "I'll bet we can find a metal detector somewhere in town and do a sweep of the parking lot when the sun is up. It'll be right as rain."

Chapter 7

Flo's Cluster Art Studio was already hopping when Aury, Scott, and Liza arrived shortly after seven in the evening. Aury was surprised at the number of people in attendance for a small town.

Mabel and Clara waved from across the room and headed their way. Their flowing skirts contained the colors Aury and her grandmother had been discussing at the winery. Mabel wore more leafy greens, while Clara emphasized the lavenders and purples.

"So glad you made it." Mabel wrapped her arms around Liza like an old friend.

"And who is this handsome man?" Clara put her arm through Scott's. "Liza, you didn't tell me you liked them so young."

Liza swiped a hand at her. "Oh, hush now. This is Aury's beau, Scott Bell."

As the ladies fussed over Scott, Aury took in the other guests. A waiter circulated with a tray of wines in three different shades. Two couples nearby accepted white wine from the tray.

"I didn't realize Songscape had sweet wine," said the gentleman with slicked-back gray hair after taking a sip.

The woman at his right elbow agreed. "I don't remember tasting anything like this when we were there last weekend. It's tasty."

The shorter man swirled the wine in his glass and held it up to the light. Aury wondered what he was looking for.

"Maybe the winery is saving the official release of this wine until after the festival, so it's not on the menu yet. We're getting a sneak preview." The second woman raised her glass in a toast. "To Songscape coming up with a sweet wine. Best of luck at the festival!"

The others clinked glasses with her.

Aury turned her attention back to her group with a small smile. It was wonderful to see Ethan's wine appreciated.

As Mabel and Clara guided them to a table, Aury took note of others appreciating the good wine and good company. She liked the small-town feel. It was one of the reasons she loved living at Eastover.

"It's really easy." Clara set a small, white canvas in front of Aury while Mabel pulled out a chair for her. "Here are your paints. When they get started, Flo will take you through the basics step by step. Mabel, get Liza an easel."

"Oh, no thank you. I'll stick with quilting. Paint was never my forte. But Scott may want to give it a go."

He held up both hands to put that idea to bed. "I see Harold from the hardware store. I have a few questions for him. Do you mind?" he asked Aury.

"Go. Have fun." She kissed him on the cheek before he wandered off.

Two women jostled past him as he worked his way toward the food table. Ruthanne spotted Aury and Liza first. "How wonderful! We didn't get a chance to get to know each other at the quilt shop the other day." She heaved herself into the seat next to Aury, dropping her purse on the ground at her feet.

Naomi nodded hello as she also found a seat. Her dashiki was loose with a plunging neckline and short sleeves. The brilliant oranges, tans, and greens set off Naomi's glowing black skin tone.

"What a wonderful dress," Liza said. "Did you make it yourself?"

Naomi held out her arms to display the pattern. "I did.

45

Thank you. These women don't appreciate my style."

"What do you ladies think of our town? Are you having a good vacation?" Ruthanne picked at the selection of foods from her overflowing plate.

Aury smiled easily. "Scott and I went hiking today around Watkins Glen. It was beautiful. Treasure loved it too."

Naomi raised her eyebrows. "Treasure?"

"Our puppy. We needed to get her away from the winery to give Joyce and Ethan's dog Elvis a break."

"Where *are* Ethan and Joyce? I can't wait to try their wine tonight," Ruthanne said.

"Joyce had a faculty event at the college, so they couldn't make it." Aury considered the selection of paint colors. She had always relished matching fabrics to make a quilt pop with the right tones but had never tried her hand at mixing paints. She was excited to get started.

"Chantel! Chantel! Over here!" Ruthanne waved both flabby arms over her head like she was guiding an airplane landing.

Clicking across the floor in her four-inch heels, Chantel rolled her eyes but headed toward their table. She shifted a large wicker purse from one arm to the other as she parted the increasing crowd. She set it on the floor with a clink.

"Isn't this a perfect table?" Ruthanne said. "We'll be able to see everything. I've been wanting to try this technique. It's so fun; no one will be able to tell if I make a mistake." She giggled.

Naomi picked up a stack of eight-inch by eight-inch canvases from the center of the table and passed them around. Tabletop easels propped the canvases so they could be worked on, but the artist could still see over the top. Liza declined again but sorted through the variety of paint colors available.

"What are we supposed to be making this time?" Chantel asked in a bored voice.

"Giraffes!" Naomi held up an example painting of an animal barely resembling a giraffe with its nose smushed against a camera lens. The color palette didn't help in its identification. Reds, blues, yellows, and greens didn't blend so much as run into each other on the canvas.

"How can anyone think that's a giraffe?" Chantel declared.

"It's pop art," explained Ruthanne. "It's about color and fun. You have to go with it."

"My ancestors would be turning over in their graves." Chantel sniffed and pushed her canvas away.

"Gran loves researching ancestry. Do you have painters in your lineage?" Aury asked.

Chantel eyed her as if noticing Aury and Liza for the first time. "The French are famous for their painters."

"Too bad you didn't inherit that gene, huh, Chantel?" Clara said.

Naomi stifled a laugh, covering it with a cough.

"Let's get some wine!" Mabel grabbed a passing waiter and snagged glasses for the table.

Liza and Aury exchanged glances at the swift change of subject.

Chantel produced two bottles from her oversized purse. "I brought a sample from my vineyard, just for our table." She looked sideways at Aury. "No offense to Songscape. I'm sure they're adequate, but I'm not in the mood for sharp wines."

"I was going to get the Riesling earlier, but someone said it was sweet. I don't care for sweet wines." Ruthanne popped a cherry tart into her mouth.

Chantel deftly removed the cork with her personal corkscrew and poured wine around the table.

Aury had to admit the wine was very good. "What grape is this?"

Chantel held her glass up to the light. "Pinot Noir is very prominent in this area. This vintage was aged in oak for three years. You can taste the earthy flavor mixed with cherries."

The ladies all sipped again.

Aury shrugged. "I don't taste it."

"Good wine is wasted on people who don't have discerning tongues." Chantel turned her back on Aury and searched the crowd. "I need to powder my nose." She picked up her purse and disappeared into the crowd.

"Don't mind her, honey." Naomi put a kind hand on Aury's arm. "Chantel is French and has aristocratic airs about wines."

"French, my ass," Clara mumbled.

"Now, now, Clara. Let's not start that again." Mabel dropped her voice to explain to Aury and Liza. "Chantel constantly reminds everyone about her French background but has never produced any proof. Christee is her married name, and she's never told anyone her maiden name. By the looks of her, I'd say it was more likely she has Native American blood."

Liza skimmed the gathering, mostly clustered around the food and wine tables. "Is her husband here?"

Ruthanne shook her head. "He died about eight years back. I think it was a heart attack."

"I thought he choked to death," Naomi said.

"No, it was a stroke." Clara upended her glass, finishing it off. "Bottom line, he may have been French, but I doubt she is. Besides, what's it matter? It's not like that gives her a leg up on winemaking."

"She does make spectacular wines. She's won the wine festival the last three years." Ruthanne poured herself another glass and topped off Naomi's.

"Ah, but this year Songscape Winery is going to give her a run for her money." Naomi took a large swallow.

Aury was proud of her soon-to-be cousins. She wouldn't feel bad at all if Ethan's wine knocked Chantel off her high horse. A familiar figure caught her eye near the makeshift bar. Matthew stood awkwardly, listening to someone Aury couldn't see around the art displays. He tugged at his shirt, ensuring it was tucked in, then nodded.

His eyes kept flicking to the display stand in front of him. Finally, he stepped forward and straightened the frame. When he stepped back, he looked more relaxed. His hand reached out again, accepting something from his companion and shoving it deep into his pants' pocket. As he turned to go out the back, Chantel materialized around the display. She caught Aury's eye, then looked away.

Flo stood on a stool and clinked a fork on her wine glass. "We're going to start painting soon, so find a seat. Those of you who just came for the food and drink, just keep your chewing down and don't spill in the paints."

There was a polite ripple of laughter.

"Let's have some fun tonight. It's easy; I promise. You don't have to use the colors I use. They are just suggestions to get you started. I hope you are enjoying Songscape's *Look What You Made Me Do* Cabernet Franc, *That's Life* Chardonnay, and *Jesus, Take the Wheel* Riesling. Ethan and Joyce couldn't make it tonight but, when you see them, make sure you let them know what a great job they're doing. Now let me refill my glass, and we'll begin."

Chantel snorted into her wine glass as she slid back into her seat, but Aury chose to ignore her rudeness.

Thankfully, many people were interested in learning from Flo, so the room was fairly attentive, and Aury was able to concentrate. Scott came by a few times to check on her, bringing her food she hardly touched. Then he retreated to the sidewalk in front of the studio where overflow tables and chairs had been set up for those not artistically inclined. Liza refilled paints for everyone around the table but mostly kept her comments to herself.

As with so many things, when Aury got involved with a task, she lost herself in it to the exclusion of all else. She barely noticed as other people began packing up for the night.

Naomi's voice finally cut through her concentration. "Honey, that is just worlds of adorable!"

Aury cocked her head sideways, looking at her painting from a different angle. "It's okay, but it's off somehow."

"Girl, it's supposed to be not quite right! That's the point of this style. Flo, come take a look at this." Naomi gestured to the hostess.

Flo took one look and clapped her hands in delight.

49

"You've got it, Aury! You did a great job overlapping the colors without letting them become blended. What do you think of this painting technique? Did you have fun?"

Aury finally put her brush back in the water. "It was fun. Thank you for putting this together."

"It was my pleasure. All proceeds tonight go to charity, so it was for a great cause." Flo was summoned to another table to ooh and ahh over someone else's work.

Liza put her arm around Aury and studied her painting. "It really is good. This could be a fun project for Eastover. You could do some of the artwork yourself. Think of all the whacky animals you could paint. You can create your own zoo."

"Let's see what Scott thinks first." Aury cleaned up her work area and carried her paintbrushes and dirty water to the utility sink in the back of the studio.

Empty wine bottles were stacked in boxes along the back hallway. *I would call that a successful night,* Aury thought.

Chapter 8

1767 Kaintwakon

"Take what I offer you. Five stones is a good trade." Kaintwakon pushed the stones toward his playmate.

"I can get my own stones. Why do I need yours?" Atohi pushed the stones back.

The nine-year-old crossed his arms. "These are special stones with the power of the Creator. You White men don't have anything so powerful. These take away fevers and bring rains during the growing season."

The smaller boy stared at him, openmouthed. "We don't have stones that do that."

"White men don't know that."

"But you can't say it if it isn't true."

"The French promise all manner of things that aren't true." Kaintwakon shoved the stones, and one rolled off their makeshift table.

Atohi flung his arm across the flat rock, sending the rest of the stones flying. "Why do I always have to play the part of the French? I want to be the one who brings honor to our Nation by discovering new goods. Let's switch places."

"Your father is not the one selected by the clan mother to interact with wily White men. You must be smart to know when they are telling the truth and when they are speaking falsely."

Jumping to his feet, Atohi took up a fighting stance. "Are you saying I'm not smart?"

"What is this now?" Hasanoanda's looming presence cast a shadow over the young boys.

Kaintwakon got to his feet. "We were just playing, Father."

"It didn't look like play, and it sounded like angry voices."

The boys were reluctant to speak.

"Kaintwakon?"

"I'm trying to teach Atohi how to trade. It's good practice for us to learn how to deal with White men."

"But it was a bad trade, and Kaintwakon is making false claims." Atohi glared at the older boy in defiance.

"Is this true, Kaintwakon?" his father asked.

The young boy was wise enough to be chastened. Only insane people spouted lies; it was a sign of a disease, and those people were to be pitied. The word of an *Onandowaga* warrior was not something to trifle with.

He hung his head. "It was a foolish game."

Hasanoanda regarded the two boys carefully. He pulled a leather thong from the pouch hanging around his waist. "Give me your right arms."

Although frightened of what was to come, the boys did not dare disobey. They held out their right arms.

Kaintwakon's father fashioned two loops and tied one end of the thong to his son's wrist and the other end to Atohi's, leaving them not more than six inches between. "You will stay like this until you learn how to work together. Visit both your mothers to see what chores need to be done."

The boys glanced at each other and then at the binding. It was going to be awkward to even walk in this position, let alone get work done.

"Yes, Father." Kaintwakon tugged at his friend, and they shuffled off.

Chapter 9

Present day

The sound of gunshots split the night. Aury sat bolt upright in bed. Scott was already pulling on his jeans before Aury had a chance to say anything. She threw off the covers and grabbed the thick terrycloth robe tossed over the armchair. Pulling it on, she followed Scott as he quietly opened the door to their room. Treasure yipped and growled, running circles around them.

A few more loud cracks, and Liza peeked out her door. "Should we call the police?" she whispered.

"What if it's a hunter? Let's call Ethan first. I don't want to cause any unnecessary attention for him," Scott suggested.

Aury carried the puppy back into their room, returning with her cellphone stuck to her ear. Treasure whined behind the closed door. "It's going straight to voicemail. I'll try Joyce." A moment later, she hung up the phone. "No luck. It's only eleven o'clock. They're probably still at the party."

"I don't hear anything downstairs. Wait here and I'll go check it out," said Scott.

Aury gave him a withering look. "Now when have you ever seen that work out well on the big screen?"

He kissed her quickly. "At least stay behind me then."

Aury reached back for her grandmother's hand.

They crept to the landing overlooking the tasting room,

and all was dark. Only the emergency lights illuminating the exits cast their red glow to the chunky furniture.

As they descended the stairs, no other shots rang out. At the bottom, Scott clicked on the overhead light. Aury covered her eyes from the sudden brightness. As her sight adjusted, she glanced around the room. Nothing was out of place. It was clean and ready for the morning visitors.

Aury had no idea where Scott had picked up a trumpet, but he was now brandishing it as a weapon. She stared intently as a disheveled Matthew with an untucked shirt peered around the corner.

Scott lowered the instrument and stepped forward. "What are you doing here this late?"

Timidly, Megan appeared behind Matthew, holding the back of his shirt tails. Her t-shirt almost reached her midthighs, and her legs were bare.

Scott's face turned red. "Oh, okay." He hung his weapon back on the wall where it had been displayed with other old musical instruments.

"So you heard it too?" Aury asked the young couple.

They nodded.

"Was it gunshots?" Liza asked.

"I guess it could have been old-man Reese, but it didn't sound like a hunting rifle to me. Besides, who hunts this late at night?" Matthew turned to Megan. "I'm going to check the doors. Why don't you go back to your room?"

For a moment, it looked like she was going to protest but then seemed to recognize her state of undress. She squealed in embarrassment and ran down the hallway.

In unspoken agreement, the remaining four split up and inspected the doors and windows. Everything was locked tight. Aury shook the handle to the bottling rooms below. It was also locked. "Do you think we should check downstairs?"

"Only Ethan has the key." Matthew went behind the main tasting bar and produced flashlights. He handed one to Scott. "Let's check the outside doors."

While the men were outside, Aury pulled a bottle from the

small wine refrigerator under the bar. She poured liquid into four mugs and carried them into the kitchen down the hall. Two minutes later, she returned with steaming mulled wine. "Don't tell Joyce I warmed it in the microwave. It's probably a grave sin in wine country."

"She won't hear it from me." Liza took the mug and sat at one of the wooden tables. The ladies watched the beams bob up and down as the men walked the property. When they approached the front door into the winery, automatic lights activated, bathing the entrance and part of the patio.

Aury rushed to unlock the door for them.

"Doors are all locked downstairs." Scott secured the door behind them. "No lights on at Ethan and Joyce's house, and her car isn't parked out front."

"What should we do?" Liza handed Scott and Matthew each a warm mug of wine.

"Nothing to do tonight. We'll talk to Ethan about it in the morning. It was probably a hunter." Scott took a sip and sighed. "Perfect."

"I'll go check on Megan." Matthew took his mug with him.

Scott pulled out a chair and sat. Locking his fingers behind his head, he stared at the ceiling, his eyes darting as if he were looking for something. A deep crease appeared between his brows.

Aury regarded Scott intently. "What is it? What aren't you saying?"

He leaned forward and rested his elbows on the table. "I thought I saw someone on the lake. It's dark down there, but the moon's out. All I could make out was a figure. It looked like a person standing on the lake."

"*On* the lake?" Liza said.

"Crazy, right? But they didn't appear to be on the bank, blending in with the trees. Is there a dock down there?"

"I don't remember. We'll have to look closer tomorrow. What did Matthew think it was?" Aury asked.

"He didn't see it. By the time I got his attention to point it out, the person was gone. Or whatever it was."

"It was the Wandering Chief."

The trio jumped when Megan spoke. She walked closer, now dressed in baggy sweats with her hair pulled up in a messy bun. Her feet were still bare, and she was cradling Matthew's mug of mulled wine in both hands. She leaned against the bar.

"Megan, honey, what are you talking about?" Liza asked.

Matthew returned, his shirt neatly tucked, and his hair combed. He rubbed Megan's back gently.

Megan spoke in a singsong voice as if she were telling ghost stories around a campfire. "Young Agayenthah was the tallest and bravest of all the Seneca warriors. One day while hunting, he wandered into an area that was forbidden to hunt. Lightning struck a tree near where he was standing, and he and the tree were thrown into the lake. The Creator swallowed Agayenthah as punishment for his disregard of the code. He must ride the lake for a thousand years as a warning to others."

She took a shaky sip of her drink. "The sounds we heard earlier must have been the voice of the Creator cursing the warrior for doing things he was not allowed to do."

Aury shuddered involuntarily. The tone of Megan's eerie voice convinced Aury that Megan truly believed what she was saying.

Liza leaned forward in her chair. "Wait, I thought it was the sea serpent that lived in a cave connecting Seneca Lake to Cayuga Lake calling for a mate."

Aury gave her grandmother an incredulous look. "Where did you get that?"

Liza waved her hand dismissively. "A book I picked up at the library about local legends."

Aury shook her head and chuckled. "Whatever it was, we aren't going to figure it out tonight." She stood and collected the mugs. "Let's chat with Ethan tomorrow and see if he has any ideas."

Megan's voice was almost a whisper. "When the warrior shows up, it means a storm is coming."

Chapter 10

The next morning, Ethan, Scott, and Aury sat around a table in the tasting room, enjoying fresh omelets and *Good Morning Mimosas*. The dogs wrestled nearby, Elvis knocking Treasure on her butt with a gentle swipe of his paw. Aury chuckled at their antics.

"I'm sorry I missed all the excitement." Ethan wiped his mouth. "I didn't even notice your call until we were on the way home, and by then it was after one in the morning. I didn't want to wake you."

"Matthew and I searched the winery, and nothing was disturbed, so we didn't call the police." Scott poured himself more coffee from the carafe on the table.

Ethan raised his eyebrows. "Matthew?" Then a look of understanding crossed his face. "Oh, I should have figured."

"How was your shindig at the college?" Aury asked.

"It was a lot of networking for Joyce. She's still getting to know these people, and she's much better at remembering names than I am. Mostly I'm arm candy."

Aury laughed at him. "Everyone has a part to play."

"What about you? Did you create a masterpiece or buy one from Flo?" Ethan asked.

"She created her own," Scott said proudly. "I can't wait to hang that crazy giraffe in my office at Eastover. It'll cheer me up every time I look at it."

Aury warmed under Scott's praise. "It was fun. Your wine was a big hit. They ran out partway through the night."

"That's good to hear. Flo bought a lot of cases. I figured I'd be picking up leftovers this morning." He pushed his chair back and picked up his dishes. "I better get to work. I want to inventory the bottles before we start the next round of crushing."

The others carried their dishes to the kitchen behind him.

"Where was Liza off to so early this morning?" Ethan asked.

Aury rolled her eyes. "She went to the library. After last night, she wanted to do more research on local legends."

"Does she ever relax?" Scott asked.

"No. I think I inherited that trait from her." Aury ran water in the sink. "You all go on. I'll help Megan open up."

Aury hummed a tune in her head from *Singin' in the Rain* while she worked. Voices interrupted her thoughts, and she cut off the water. *Is that yelling?* She thought it might be coming from downstairs. Quickly drying her hands, she ran to the deck facing the large vats. More cursing came from the bottling room. She raced toward Ethan's voice.

When she entered the large room, she stopped suddenly. Glass shards littered the floor. The smell of wine hung in the air, and sunlight from the open barn door reflected off the red liquid covering the tile. "What happened?"

Ethan was still muttering and cursing to himself.

"Some of the bottles burst," Scott explained quietly. "That's probably what we heard last night."

"Oh, Ethan, I'm sorry. What could have caused that?" Aury asked.

He ran a hand through his hair. "I must have mixed it wrong. Maybe the fermentation wasn't complete when I bottled these. But I know I tested them." He shook his head. "This was my Cab Franc for the upcoming wine festival. They've been down here for nine months. Why would they pop now?" He regarded the room as if the answer would jump out at him. He sighed. "I'll get the broom. Then we can hose down the floors."

Aury left them to clean up and went back upstairs to finish the breakfast dishes.

When the front door chime announced a visitor, Aury put the last plate away and went out to greet the guest. The sheriff had removed his hat and was impatiently tapping it against his leg.

"Good morning, sheriff. Are you looking for breakfast? They don't start serving for another half hour, but I can probably whip up eggs for you. I make a mean omelet."

He eyeballed her up and down. "And you are?"

She offered her hand. "I'm sorry. I'm Aury St. Clair. My fiancée is Ethan's cousin."

He shook her hand. "Is Ethan around? I'd like to talk to him."

"Sure. I'll get him. He and Scott are cleaning a mess in the bottling room. Have a seat." Aury's imagination spun. *Maybe there was more to the shots we heard last night.*

When Aury returned with Ethan and Scott, the sheriff stood in the same spot where she had left him. Elvis and Treasure had come to inspect the newcomer, but he ignored them.

Ethan shook hands with him and introduced Scott. "Sheriff Dines, what can I help you with?"

The sheriff glanced between Ethan and Scott. "It's not raining. Why are you wet?"

The vineyard owner inspected his shoes and trousers. "I had a problem in the bottling room. We were hosing things down."

"Problem with the wine?" The sheriff looked skeptical.

"As a matter of fact, yes. What do you need, officer?" Ethan's tone had changed from friendly to wariness, matching that of the sheriff's.

"Were you at the Cluster Art Studio night for Flo's event?"

"No, I wasn't." He gestured to Scott. "My cousin and Aury were there though. Why? What happened?"

"Isn't it a little peculiar that you didn't attend an event where your wines were featured so prominently?"

"Sheriff, I'm a businessman. I don't hang out at restaurants where they serve my wines either. Joyce had an event for work. We were at the college."

Dines focused on the couple. "Are you feeling all right this morning?"

"That's an odd question," Aury said. "Yes, we're fine. What's this about?"

Reluctantly, Dines explained. "There was trouble at the Cluster last night. Some people got pretty sick. Ended up in the hospital. One person didn't make it."

"Didn't make it to the hospital?" She was confused.

"Didn't live."

The air was sucked out of Aury's lungs. She sank into a nearby seat.

Even the men were stunned into silence.

"Who died?" Aury asked weakly.

Dines shook his head. "We aren't releasing that information yet."

"Of course," she mumbled.

The sheriff went on with his questions. "How late did you stay?"

Scott shrugged. "Almost to the end. We helped clean up a bit. Moved the furniture back inside. That kind of thing."

"Did you drink the wine?" Dines's eyes narrowed.

"I didn't. I was designated driver." Scott took Aury's hand.

"Sure, while I was painting. I didn't get drunk or anything." Aury didn't like where these questions were going. "Why do you think it had anything to do with the wine?"

"Seems to be the common denominator, is all. People drinking the wine got sick. People who didn't were fine. How is it you didn't get sick?" His gaze landed on Aury.

Chantel's wine bag popped into Aury's head, but she held her tongue. She didn't want to admit she wasn't drinking Ethan's wine, because Chantel had brought her own. Aury was relieved her grandmother hadn't had anything to drink at the party. With her medication, Gran strictly limited herself to one glass a night, and that she had at the winery before they left.

"I'm not sure. But how could wine possibly make anyone that sick?"

"That's what we're trying to figure out." Dines turned to Ethan. "Do you have any of the wine you sold to Flo left? Seems they ran out last night."

Ethan's face paled. "I'll have to check the ticket to see what we sent over. She had a variety."

"I'll wait."

Ethan went to his office.

"Could it have been food poisoning? Maybe something had been left out too long," Aury said.

"Did you eat the food?" Dines asked.

Aury shook her head. "I was so focused on painting, I barely touched anything."

"I ate her share," admitted Scott. "The food was great."

"Regardless, by the time we realized people were getting sick, Flo's studio had been cleaned up and any remaining food was dumped. The trash was collected this morning. That's why we don't have any bottles left to check either." Dines tapped his hat on his leg a few more times impatiently.

"We almost called you last night." Aury shot a look at Scott. "When we were in bed, we heard the bottles explode—of course we didn't know what it was at the time. It sounded a little like gunshots. When Scott went out to investigate, he saw someone on the lake."

"That's not unusual. Lots of people use the lake." The sheriff scanned the tasting room.

"In the middle of the night?"

"That's their prerogative." He focused on Scott. "What did you see?"

Scott reddened under his examination. "Just a figure on the lake. He was standing. I didn't see a boat."

"It was a he?"

Scott shrugged. "Actually, I couldn't really tell. They were thin and held an item in their hand, like a staff. The moon was behind him—them—so I only saw a silhouette."

"Your imagination probably conjured up the ghost of the lake. Happens all the time to newcomers."

"I hadn't even heard of the Seneca warrior until after I saw it," Scott said. "Megan told us the story last night."

Ethan returned with a copy of the receipt. If possible, he was even whiter than before. "One of the batches that Flo bought was from the wine we were cleaning up downstairs. The bottles burst last night."

"Let's take a look."

The two men went downstairs. Scott retrieved coffee from the kitchen and sat with Aury, handing her a cup.

A few minutes later, Liza fluttered through the doorway, cheeks rosy, her arms full of books. "Wait 'til you see what I found. There's a logical explanation for those sounds we heard last night." She trailed off when she caught sight of Aury's face. She rushed to her side, dumping the books on the table. "Are you all right?"

Aury's face burned with anger that Ethan could be accused of something so horrible. She stood and began to pace, her thoughts racing for another explanation to feed the sheriff.

"What is it, child?" Liza guided Aury back down and sat in the chair next to her. She took her hands. Treasure put her small paws on Aury's knees, lending her comforting support.

Petting Treasure absentmindedly, Aury filled Liza in on what the sheriff had told them and about the exploding wine bottles. "He's in the basement now with Ethan. I think he imagines Ethan was trying to get rid of evidence."

"Don't you worry none. The sheriff's got to do his job, but he'll see Ethan wouldn't hurt a flea."

Scott cleared his throat. "What if it was unintentional? What if the mixing was just wrong and made these people sick?"

"Pahhh." Liza dismissed the notion. "We've been here for days, drinking wine practically at every meal. If it was Ethan's wine, we would have gotten sick. There must be another explanation."

Aury rolled that over in her mind. "The dying vines, exploding bottles, nails in the parking lot. And now sick partygoers. Whatever's going on here, we have to figure out how these pieces fit together."

"Don't forget the furniture being moved about and the ghost on the lake," Liza offered.

A shiver ran up Aury's spine. Ever since her parents died in a car crash five years ago, she was acutely sensitive to the needs of others. Her parents had been on the way to her house to comfort her after another fight with her now-ex-husband when the drunk driver hit them. For years afterward, Aury was overcome with guilt. These days, she transferred that guilt into determination. That drive helped her get to the bottom of things.

Megan strolled out from behind the bar. "Good morning. Have you eaten already, or do you want me to fix you pancakes?"

Aury peered past Megan's shoulder, looking for Matthew.

Answering Aury's unasked question, Megan blushed. "Matthew went home last night. We were trying to keep things on the down-low, but I guess our secret's out."

Offering a wan smile, Aury said, "We've eaten. Thank you."

"I'll get the kitchen set up for the morning then." Megan disappeared into the back room.

"I saw Matthew at Flo's party. I wonder why he was there. He was talking to Chantel." Aury spoke more to herself than to Scott and Liza.

"Don't let your imagination run away with itself," Scott cautioned.

"I think you're on to something." Liza thoughtfully tapped her chin.

Scott made a face. "Liza, don't encourage her."

She ignored him, digging through her pocketbook for a

pen and sticky pads. "We need to make a list of inquiries to figure this out."

The sheriff and Ethan came back up the stairs; the sheriff held a bottle in a plastic evidence bag. "I'll have this tested and let you know what we find."

Ethan appeared miserable and simply nodded.

Dines peered at Aury and Scott. "You going to be in town for a while?"

"A least a week. We came up for the festival," Scott answered.

Dines put his hat on as he departed.

"What does he think he's going to find?" Aury asked.

"Poison, I assume." Ethan buried his hands in his pockets, staring at the floor.

"Why would you poison your own wine? That doesn't make any sense." Scott shook his head.

"He hinted that it could have been accidental because I'm new at this."

"That's ridiculous," Liza said.

"Is it? I was speculating the same thing about why the bottles exploded. I must have processed it wrong. Why else would they burst?"

"We'll get to the bottom of this. Don't you worry." Aury's heart was heavy in her chest.

Ethan slumped toward the kitchen. "I need to call Joyce and let Megan know I'm not going to open up today. Until we figure this out, I don't feel safe serving my wines."

Chapter 11

Only moments passed before Megan dashed out of the kitchen and to her car. She looked frightened, but Aury suspected that was a common occurrence for her. If her storytelling was any indication, Megan leaned toward the dramatic. Aury predicted she would seek out Matthew. Scott and Ethan returned to the bottling room.

Liza drummed her pen on the table. "Who would benefit from Ethan's wine being bad?"

"Any of the other wineries, I guess." Aury shifted to stare out the glass patio window to the grapevines below. "But there are many wineries around here. What does one more matter? If someone stooped to poisoning whenever another one opened, this wouldn't be such a surprise. Besides, this was a winery before. It's not totally new."

"What about that old man? I don't like the sight of *Rodney Reese*." Liza practically spat out his name.

Aury answered slowly. "He may be a grouch, but he's lived here his whole life. Would he really take his grudge over losing the land to Ethan out on innocent people?"

Liza pointed her pen at Aury. "You caught him snooping around the bottling room. Maybe he tainted them somehow."

"But he helped with the soil sample. It won't do him any good to win the land back from Ethan if it comes with a bad reputation. He won't be able to turn a profit in what's left of his lifetime."

They sat in thoughtful silence.

"Matthew's a bit quirky, and I don't mean his nervous ticks. Why was he at the Cluster last night? And why was he meeting up with Chantel? What did she give him?" Aury mulled the idea over.

Liza wrote furiously as Aury spoke. Then she wrote Chantel and underlined it. "Maybe it isn't all the wineries. Chantel has won the festival competition for the last several years. Maybe she doesn't like Ethan gaining ground on her."

"How would Chantel have access to the bottling room?" Aury asked.

"Maybe that's why she was with Matthew! She was paying him to do her dirty work." Liza's eyes grew excited. "Maybe they're in it together."

"Who's in what together?" Scott entered from downstairs, Ethan right behind him.

Liza and Aury exchanged guilty glances. "We're only brainstorming," Aury said. "We're not accusing anyone of anything."

"I should hope not." Ethan went behind the bar to wash his hands. "This whole mess may just be a horrible accident."

"How well do you know Chantel Christee?" Liza asked.

"From Chateau Christee? Not well. I've met her at functions. The gentleman who sold me this place recommended her as a good source if I ever have questions."

An idea materialized before Aury. "Have you turned to her for advice? Maybe she pointed you the wrong way on purpose."

Ethan chuckled. "I think you're reaching. I've never talked about wine with Chantel. Joyce has connections at Cornell, so if I get stuck, I turn to them. They haven't steered me wrong yet."

Scott peeked over Liza's shoulder. "Come on. Who else is on your list?"

Liza instinctively covered the paper, then seemed to think better of it and moved her hands. Sharing with Scott was inevitable.

He read the scratchy handwriting. "You're right that Matthew had the biggest opportunity to tamper with bottles— if they were tampered with—but what motive would he have?"

Ethan considered the question. "He wanted to put a bid on the winery when it went up for sale, but Matthew's too young to qualify for such a hefty loan. I'm not sure the previous owner ever took him seriously."

"That might have made him angry enough to lash out." Liza stabbed the sticky note with her pen to emphasize her words.

"But why would he be mad at me?" Ethan asked. "I didn't have anything to do with his inability to get a loan. And I've given him a good job here—with a raise in pay."

"Why was he at Flo's last night?" Aury asked.

"He delivered wine earlier in the day. Maybe he forgot something." Ethan brushed it off. "He's a good worker, even if he's a bit odd."

"Why would Chantel be passing him something? Maybe it was a pay off." Liza wasn't going to let this go.

"Or maybe he dropped a piece of paper, and she picked it up for him. Let's not presume guilt prematurely. Just like I don't want people assuming I'm guilty before anything is proven, let's not persecute poor Matthew." Ethan ran a hand through his hair.

Aury wondered if he realized how often he did that when he got nervous. He'd be losing hair before too long at this rate.

He went on. "I'm going to go through my notes again and see if I can spot an error. Then I might run my journals to a professor friend at Cornell to look them over. Another set of eyes couldn't hurt."

"Do you want company?" Scott offered.

"Sure. I'll teach you how to run tests on the wine. I'd feel better if we retested every batch." He gave them both a small smile. "I don't think I've said it yet, but I'm so glad you and Aury are here. It's nice to have family to lean on."

The men left again, and Liza and Aury went back to picking apart their theories. When their brainstorming stalled, Aury asked, "How did it go at the library this morning? You didn't get a chance to fill us in."

Liza's demeanor brightened. "I found a lot about the area in the local history section. I was looking for an explanation for the noises we heard last night. Obviously, it's a moot point since we now know it was the bottles exploding, but this is fascinating anyway. The legend about the Seneca warrior Megan told us was hogwash. It came from a satirical piece written by James Fenimore Cooper in the 1800s about the American political speechmakers."

"So why do people say it's a native legend?"

"People will believe whatever is easy to repeat." Liza flipped the pages of one of the books strewn across the table. Moving a sticky note she had used to mark her place, she scanned the note she made about the page. "Cooper himself described sounds from Seneca Lake as the explosion of heavy artillery. At that time, they had no way of knowing what it was. People refer to it as the Seneca Drums."

"So what is it really?" Aury knew her grandmother would have ferreted out more information.

"Apparently, natural gas escaped from a layer of sandstone deep beneath the lake. When they floated to the top and burst, they made a booming sound."

"That's what Ethan was talking about the other day. But it didn't seem that loud. Certainly not a boom."

Liza glanced at her notes again. "When they started salt mining in this area, the gas had other outlets to escape. In the 1930s, businesses developed natural gas fields, and that pretty much put an end to the lake guns or Seneca Drums. Perhaps there are still some residual noises that keep the legends alive."

Aury rested her feet on the chair next to her. "This area is fascinating. Joyce told us about the Haudenosaunee presence in this area, but she didn't mention what happened after the colonists beat the British."

Pushing aside the book referencing the drums, Liza picked up another and read the title. Under it, she had pasted another sticky note. She read it silently, then turned to a specific page and scanned. "George Washington sent Generals Sullivan and Clinton to destroy over forty villages. They laid waste to hundreds of acres of fields and any food or materials the Haudenosaunee were storing. It's known as the Sullivan Campaign of 1779. After the war, the new United States divided the Haudenosaunee land into allotments for colonial soldiers to retire on."

"That's horrible."

"Totally senseless, if you ask me. There's plenty of land to go around. The Haudenosaunee Confederacy lived peacefully for centuries. They even traded with the French and British."

Liza picked up a different book and started flipping through it. "This is fascinating. Seneca Lake is forty miles long and three miles wide and is the second deepest lake in the United States. There's even speculation about a subterranean passage to the sea."

"Where do they get that idea?" Aury felt it was unlikely because they were so far from the ocean.

"Fishermen have caught salt-water fish in this lake, and it's tidal."

"The water level actually changes with the moon? I didn't think that happened on a lake."

Liza nodded vigorously. "It's fed by underground springs. Granted, the changes are very minor, but they are measurable."

"Great job, Gran. You should have been a librarian."

"Books and fabric. Two of my favorite things."

"Speaking of which, why don't we head into town? We can have lunch and check out the gossip," Aury suggested.

"I certainly wouldn't mind seeing what the ladies at the quilt shop are up to today. Maybe they have more details on what happened last night."

Aury stood. "It's hard to help Ethan with only some of the facts. We don't even know who died."

Chapter 12

1768 Kaintwakon

Kaintwakon worked alongside his parents, digging in the soil to introduce a new plant to this land. They already had *o:nyö ́gwi'sä'*, so he didn't understand the purpose of growing a new variety.

"Add water to these. They need a head start for their roots to firmly grab the earth." Genessee motioned for the young boy to bring the bucket.

Hasanoanda stood tall, looking over the area they had planted. "Soon enough, the lake waters will contribute to their growth. We will see if the Creator accepts this gift from the French or not."

"Why would the French give us grapevines?" Kaintwakon asked his father.

"Because they want something from us. I traded them for the beaver furs we collected last season. But what the White men don't appreciate is that those furs will not last forever. If these vines take, they will give much to our people for many generations."

Kaintwakon couldn't complain about that. He enjoyed the sweet fruit as much as the next person. Except, of course, the time he and his friends had descended on the grapes while they were still green. Thinking to get to the fruit before the birds, the boys had stuffed themselves.

While their bellies still ached, his mother had reminded him that the grapes didn't belong to the Haudenosuanee. They were a gift from the Creator. The birds should be free to take their share, and Kaintwakon was to be grateful.

Genessee patted soil around the last plant and stood. "When will you meet with the French again?"

Kaintwakon dutifully drenched the small plant with water, listening intently for his father's response.

"After the next full moon, we will meet on the northern bank of the lake. This time, they promise metal tools to make planting and harvesting easier."

His mother raised her eyebrows at this. "What can be easier than the tools we already have? They have served us well. I'm not sure continued contact with the French is worth the trinkets we get."

Hasanoanda looked at his son but spoke to Genessee. "We must share the land with the White man; I don't see another way. If we can learn to live with them, perhaps they will learn to respect our ways."

"The White men don't seem to have respect for themselves. It is unlikely they will change for us." His mother spoke softly, but her wisdom was always worth listening to.

"What you say may be true, but the Creator brought them to these hills, the same as us. We must work together for the sake of this land." Hasanoanda spread his arms toward the garden.

Listening respectfully, Kaintwakon's attention pivoted between his parents. He shifted the now-empty water bucket from one hand to the other.

"I'm concerned they do not appreciate Mother Earth. With their greed, they jeopardize the balance of the gifts she provides." Genessee turned to look at the lake.

"Maybe it is our responsibility to guide them into a better understanding of unity. How can we do that if we don't interact?" His father was making good points too.

Kaintwakon wanted to get to know the White men better. He liked receiving the tools and trinkets his father brought home. Someday, he hoped to work alongside his father and bring pride to his clan.

When Genessee was silent for a time, Hasanoanda stepped closer, pulling her stare from the lake. "I wish to take Kaintwakon with me to our next meeting."

Kaintwakon's heart leapt with joy at this news. In the past, his father had said he was too young to be at such events.

He held his breath waiting for his mother's response. She pulled out her pipe and took her time filling it with sacred tobacco from her pouch. He and Hasanoanda waited, knowing this was not something to be rushed.

Genessee closed her eyes but lifted her chin to the sky as the smoke rose. His father joined her discussion with the Creator, all the while Kaintwakon remained still.

Eventually, Genessee regarded him, but he couldn't read her eyes. *Was that sadness?*

She spoke once again to Hasanoanda. "It will be as you say."

Kaintwakon almost cheered out loud.

"But," she continued, "you must prepare him, cautioning him about the ways the French say one thing when they sometimes mean another."

Chapter 13

Present day

As Aury and Liza sat at the Lakeside Diner eating chicken salad sandwiches, their ears were attuned to conversations around them. As Aury suspected, everyone was talking about the incident at the Cluster the night prior. Of course, few of these people had actually attended the event, or they might have been home sick as well.

The stories ranged from a virus to bad wine to the curse of the Seneca Warrior. Aury needed more information, and the ladies at the quilt shop always seemed to be in the know.

Abandoning the rest of their meal, Aury and Liza paid their bill and walked to the Grape Basket Quilt Shop. The chiming bell was met with sighs of relief.

"Oh, thank goodness you're okay." Mabel hugged Aury then Liza tightly.

Clara swept in for the next round of squeezes. "We weren't sure if you had gotten sick or not."

"We're fine. Glad to see neither of you was affected," Liza said.

"How could we be? We didn't drink Songscape wine." Mabel slapped a hand over her mouth, but it was too late.

Aury's spine went rigid. "Has there been any proof that the wine was the cause of the illness? Maybe it was the food."

Clara waved away the notion. "Wine Pairing Catering

has been in the area for years. They serve the most delicious shrimp and crackers."

Mabel elbowed her in the ribs.

"Why are you elbowing me? What did I say? You were just commenting about what a lovely spread Wine Catering puts on. It's the wine we were—" This time she caught herself.

"It's just . . . you have to understand . . . we can't be sure." Mabel couldn't seem to get her words out.

"We know people got sick last night, but the sheriff didn't give many details." Liza held her pocketbook with both hands in front of her.

"Oh, did the sheriff go out to Songscape?" Mabel eyed her shrewdly.

Aury realized her grandmother's mistake. "Ethan is helping the sheriff get to the bottom of this in any way he can. He provided a sample of his wine. The lab will run tests and prove Songscape didn't have anything to do with this."

"I spoke to Chantel this morning. She's pretty shaken up but not sick. You have to admit, it's quite a coincidence that no one at our table got ill. We were only drinking the wine Chantel brought." Clara became almost apologetic.

"And why did she bring her own wine anyway?" snapped Liza.

Mabel began straightening fabric bolts on a nearby table. "That's just Chantel. She can be kind of uppity about her wines."

"Or maybe she knew there would be a problem with the Songscape wine. Did you think of that?" Liza had entered protective-mother mode. No one dare speak poorly of her children. Now, if the child had done something wrong, Aury was well aware of the wrath that would follow. Gran would always protect first, but she also didn't let children get away with anything.

"What are you accusing Chantel of?" Clara asked.

Aury placed a calming hand on her grandmother's arm. "We aren't accusing anyone of anything, but we also don't think Ethan should be accused either. Let's wait and see what the sheriff comes up with."

The bell on the door sounded, breaking the tension. Ruthanne shuffled into the shop, eyes red-rimmed from crying.

"What is it, dear?" Clara rushed forward and placed an arm around her shoulders, ushering the pale woman to a nearby chair and handing her a tissue.

Ruthanne dabbed at her eyes and blew her nose loudly. Clara handed her the box of tissues.

"I just came from Leslie's house. Her poor son . . ." She broke off in a sob.

"Kevin? What's wrong?" Clara asked.

"He's dead."

The room fell silent, except for Ruthanne's sniffling.

Mabel shook her head sympathetically; her eyes welled with tears. "He was turning into such a nice young man too."

Clara addressed Aury and Liza. "Kevin cleaned a lot of the businesses around town after hours. He did a fine job. Always on time and very trustworthy."

Liza paled. "We met him the other day."

"Leslie is beside herself. Kevin had just moved out on his own." Ruthanne tucked the used tissues into her purse.

Aury searched her memory. "I didn't see Kevin at the party last night."

Mabel shook her head. "No, no. He's only twenty and that's not his scene, but he usually cleans for Flo in the art studio."

"When Harold opened the barber shop this morning, he noticed Kevin hadn't been there. He usually leaves it spic and span. Harold called Leslie when Kevin didn't answer his phone. She went around to his apartment." Ruthanne choked back sobs. "And found him on the bathroom floor."

"That poor family," Liza murmured. "Do they have any idea what happened to him?"

"It's obvious, isn't it? First all those sick people, now

Kevin. He must have drunk the wine while he was cleaning up." All Mabel's reservations were gone now.

"You just said he wasn't at the party. I don't think there's a connection." Aury tried to calm the rising panic in the room.

Ruthanne went on as if Aury hadn't spoken. "Why didn't Flo just get Chantel's wine?" Ruthanne's words came out as a bark. "She knows Chantel's quality. Why take a chance on a newcomer and risk *this*?"

Biting back what she wanted to say, Aury took Liza's arm. "Let's go."

They left Clara and Mabel comforting Ruthanne.

On the car ride back to the winery, they were uncommonly quiet. As they were pulling in, Aury said, "I thought they ran out of Ethan's wine during the party. How did Kevin get hold of a bottle? He wasn't old enough to buy it."

"There you go. Now you're assuming it was the wine too. We don't know what made people sick."

"Why do you think Chantel brought her own wine?" Aury stared out the front windshield into the fields.

"It's like she presumed something might have been wrong with Ethan's," Liza interjected.

"She is definitely a competitive one, but to go as far as to poison people over wine? Seems pretty extreme."

They got out of the car and walked up the front path.

Inside the tasting room, Ethan paced back and forth, muttering curses. His hair was a mess from running his hands through it.

Joyce was trying to calm him down. Elvis paced alongside his human as if trying to get his attention.

"What did we miss?" Aury asked Scott. She picked up Treasure from where she was chewing on Scott's shoelaces.

"We went into town to pick up supplies. People were asking Ethan if it was true that he was going to sell the winery. Not just at one place: folks at the hardware store, the grocery store, even the gas station."

"They need to mind their own business! Where did they

get the idea I was going to sell? Why would I? Who would say that?" Ethan was still wound up.

Handing the puppy over to Scott, Aury went to the kitchen, looking for tea to help calm Ethan. After heating water in the microwave, she dropped a chamomile tea bag into the steaming mug. She stopped at the doorway to juggle the hot liquid while opening the door and shutting off the light switch. Whispered voices caught her attention. She held her breath, straining her ears to pick out the words.

"Do you hear this? If Ethan sells, I might have another shot at buying the winery." Matthew's hushed tone carried down the hallway.

"What are you talking about? You don't want this place. It's haunted. The Warrior isn't happy about what's going on here." Frustration strained Megan's voice.

Matthew scoffed at her. "When are you going to get over this ghost-thing of yours?"

"Don't you dare dismiss this warning. Ethan knows exactly what he's doing with processing the wine. He's meticulous. There's no way he made a mistake, and he certainly didn't do this on purpose. The ghost is angry and is not about to let this winery succeed. That's why Tolars sold it to Ethan so quickly. They were starting to lose money."

"You don't know that." This time, Matthew didn't sound as sure of himself.

"Of course I do. I helped with the books sometimes. The yields have been lower than expected in the north fields."

"You mean the field closest to Mr. Reese's property? I figured it was because of the animals tunneling there."

Megan exhaled loudly. "I'm telling you, nothing good is coming out of this place. I thought the cleansing I did in the tasting room would appease the ghost, but ever since you started talking about buying the winery again, things have been getting worse. Those bottles didn't randomly explode. Check which field they were from. I'll bet there's a connection. Alcohol should not be made on Seneca land."

"Plenty of wineries thrive in this area, and it all belonged to the Haudenosaunee at one point."

"There's something about this property." Her voice trailed off.

They were silent for a moment.

"I'm going to look for another place to work," Megan said finally.

"Not now! We're so close." Matthew was practically begging.

A door banged shut, louder to Aury's ears because of her intense concentration on the whispered conversation. *So close to what?* She waited to ensure Matthew and Megan were gone, then continued to the tasting room.

Joyce had gotten Ethan to sit on an overstuffed couch, but he still fidgeted, his right leg bouncing on the ball of his toe. Elvis rested his head on Ethan's lap. Subconsciously, Ethan outlined the tan patch around Elvis's right eye, then the black one around his left.

Aury set the tea on the coffee table in front of Ethan, noting that his leg had stopped jostling under Elvis's attention. She sank down in a loveseat across from them, next to Gran.

"It doesn't matter what they say. You're doing a fine job. I'm proud of you." Joyce took Ethan's hand.

Ethan's cell phone buzzed. He answered and listened for a few minutes without speaking. He hung up, muttering thanks to the caller.

Aury and the others watched him expectedly.

"The test results are back from the bottle of wine I gave the sheriff."

Chapter 14

Silence blanketed the room.

"Don't leave us hanging." Scott stood protectively close to where his cousin sat, as if trying to lend his support through proximity.

"They didn't find anything in the wine bottle that shouldn't be there. Because forensics didn't have anything to test at the Cluster, the sheriff is ruling it accidental food poisoning." Ethan's face didn't display the relief Aury expected.

"That's good news, right?" Liza asked.

"It's not a definitive answer. What if it was my wine? I still don't know for sure."

Scott patted Ethan's back. "We'll figure it out."

Ethan hung his head. "The sheriff indicated that Kevin died from the same bacteria or whatever that made the others sick. It's too much of a coincidence to think there's two different strains hitting on the same night."

"But Kevin wasn't at the party. That means it couldn't be your wine." Aury cheered at that thought.

"Is this going to put a damper on the wine festival this weekend?" Liza asked.

Ethan crossed his arms and leaned back into the couch cushion. "I should drop out."

Joyce rested her head on his shoulder. "No, don't do that. It's like admitting defeat."

Aury agreed. "Besides, the sheriff said it was food

poisoning. If you don't show up, it'll be like telling everyone that it was your wine. This town is small. A rumor like that could shut you down."

"She has a point," Scott said.

"But I was planning on entering one of the wines I gave to Flo. Now people won't touch it." Ethan sighed.

Liza slapped her hands on the coffee table. "So, let's select a different one."

After a little coaxing, Ethan pulled four different bottles from the bottling room. Two had not been released to the public yet, but two were from last year's bottling. Joyce begged out of the tasting. She was meeting with the dean of her department and didn't think it would be wise to show up with wine on her breath.

Ethan kissed Joyce lightly. "I know you have to go to work. Thanks for being here."

She waved goodbye on her way out, promising not to be too late.

He lined the bottles up from dry to sweet and called the others to join him at the bar. "Are you sure you want to do this? We still don't know for sure what caused those people to get sick."

"Ethan, we trust you. We've been drinking wine here all week and we're fine." As if to prove her point, Aury held up a wine glass to be served.

He sighed, then tried to put on his showman's face as he launched into vintner mode. "I don't have any truly sweet wines. I usually stick with semi-dry. At least until I figure out how to produce a good dessert wine with a late harvest."

"What about the Riesling served at Flo's?" Liza turned to Aury. "Didn't Ruthanne say it was sweet?"

Ethan shook his head. "*Jesus, Take the Wheel* could be described as semi-sweet at best. It tends more toward the drier side. That's why I picked it for the wine festival. Sweet wines are not usually considered as good to refined palettes."

Before they sampled, Ethan explained each wine in turn, highlighting the floral notes and telling them the best food pairing. He started with a red wine. "This goes well with steak, preferably cooked rare to medium. The peppery taste in the wine brings out the best in the meat."

The group dutifully sipped. Aury tasted the pepper Ethan mentioned, as well as something else. *Smoke? How do you taste smoke?*

As he poured a glass of white, he said, "You should be able to note a subtle taste of green apple with a hint of cinnamon."

Aury closed her eyes and sipped. She was surprised she could taste the apple, although it wasn't strong. She wondered how much of that was from the subliminal hints Ethan placed in her head. "Don't tell us what we should taste this time and let's see if we can figure it out."

Ethan smiled and poured another wine. They each sipped, then sipped again.

Liza spoke first. "I taste something green."

In her laughter, Aury almost choked on her wine. "You taste green? What does that even mean?"

Her grandmother slapped her lightly on the arm. "Well, I don't know. This is a new experience. I'm trying."

"Actually, she isn't far off." Ethan picked up his glass and swirled it. "Stick your nose in the glass and take a deep sniff."

They followed his lead.

"Now sip, but don't swallow it right away. Let it rest on your tongue. Think about the different areas it's hitting. Do you notice it more in the front or the back?"

They continued through the tasting process. Ethan guided them in what to focus on and how to get the most from their tasting experience. He had learned a lot in the short time he had been a vintner. Aury was impressed.

"Of course, it really comes down to what you like. It doesn't matter how many medals it has; if you don't like the taste, you shouldn't buy it." Ethan capped the last bottle and set it aside. "So what do you think? Which one should I enter in the festival?"

"Chardonnay," they all answered together, then burst out laughing.

"Guess that's my answer. Hands down." Ethan grinned broadly. "Thanks for the help and the encouragement. This will be the first time I've entered any of my wines in a competition. I'm not sure how I feel about being judged."

Aury patted his hand. "It's the wine, not you personally. It'll be great. You'll see."

A worried look crossed Ethan's face.

Aury could only imagine what he was thinking about. "Why don't we take the dogs for a walk and get some fresh air?"

Ethan shook himself out of his thoughts. "Sounds good."

Liza elected to rest while Aury, Scott, and Ethan walked the property. The dogs romped and rolled in the grass. Ethan's temperament improved as he explained his plans for the next stages of the winery.

When they neared the house, a truck pulled into the parking lot. A man about their age got out wearing a Cornell sweatshirt and raggedy blue jeans.

"Zachary, you didn't have to come all the way out here. I would have come to you." Ethan shook his hand and introduced the others.

"I wanted to see where the magic happened. But I have bad news for you." Jeffery handed Ethan a stapled packet of papers. "Your soil sample came back. You've got chemicals that shouldn't be there."

"What? How's that possible?" Ethan flipped through the pages.

"I thought you already had the soil tested and it was good." Aury looked from Ethan to Jeffery.

"That was the sample Rodney ran. When things weren't improving, I decided to go to the Cornell labs." Ethan turned to Zachary. "So what is this? How could it have gotten into the soil?"

"It's manmade, I'm afraid. It had to be deliberately added."

Ethan cursed under his breath.

"The good news is that it's a non-chlorinated pesticide

that we can counteract through bioremediation," Zachary quickly added. "It might take a while, but we'll introduce micro-organisms including bacteria and fungi that will eat away at the contaminants. I've got my students working on it. In a few months, you'll be good as new."

"In time for next year's crop?" Ethan asked hopefully.

"I don't see why not. I think you caught it early enough."

The men shook hands again.

"Thanks for all your help. The wine's on me for you and your students—if they're twenty-one." Ethan held up a finger for emphasis.

Scott asked, "What happened with the first sample?"

"Rodney must have faked the results." Aury's mind was racing. "Maybe he's the one who poisoned your vines."

"But why? He's a mean old goat, but I don't think he'd stoop to this. I need to call Joyce and let her know." Ethan smacked the pages against his open palm.

"Maybe this is a bad time for a tour," Zachary said.

Ethan shook his head. "No, please. I'd love to show you around. Let's start in the crushing room."

"What are you thinking?" Scott asked Aury, when the two men walked away.

"Rodney wanted to buy this land when Tolars sold it. Maybe he's trying to make it unusable to Ethan, so he'll sell. Let's walk down there."

The ground around the vines was still raised in patches, but Treasure didn't attempt to dig. She sniffed around, then chased a butterfly who flew within her range.

Scott stepped on a mound. "I don't see any new tunnels, but I didn't count them last time."

Aury gauged the distance between the end of the row and Reese's property line and fruit trees. Nothing but a thin wire on posts separated the fields.

"Haven't you two got a home to go to?" Reese's gravelly voice interrupted her thoughts.

"Mr. Reese." Scott's tone was cold, bordering on rude.

Rodney ducked his head under the wire and stomped his

way across the distance. "I see them vines aren't getting any better. You let your cousin know I can take this problem off his hands, seeing as he's looking to sell."

Scott clenched his hands and tried to remain calm. "He's not selling, thank you."

"That's not the way I hear it." Rodney spit in the dirt.

"You had your buddy run the soil sample from this area, didn't you?" Aury asked.

"You know I did. The problem with them vines isn't the soil. Must be the tending."

"Ethan had another sample run. Someone poisoned this field." Aury watched him closely.

Rodney reacted as if slapped. "Not possible. Jeb runs all my tests. He said it's clean as a whistle."

"Or maybe he told you something different, but you lied to Ethan." She bit off her words.

"Doesn't make any sense for me to poison this field." Rodney shook his head. "It butts up against my orchard. Anything dumped here can leach into my trees. That's no good for me. Besides, I offered to buy up this property. Why would I do that if it was bad?"

"Why didn't your guy catch the foreign chemicals in the soil?" Scott asked.

"I ran the soil I was given. Maybe Ethan don't know how to even take a right soil sample." He shook a dirty finger in their direction. "You tell that upstart he had better get this cleaned up before it affects my fields or he's going to have a nasty lawsuit on his hands. I'm going to have my soil tested right away."

Treasure turned her attention from the butterfly and ran toward the old man, barking protectively.

He raised a foot as if to kick the pup.

"Don't you dare!" Aury snapped. She rushed forward and gathered Treasure into her arms.

The dog continued to bark as Reese stormed back across the property line.

Aury and Scott watched him go.

"Matthew's the one who took the soil sample. Could he have done it wrong?" Scott wondered aloud.

"Or switched it on purpose." Aury thought about Matthew's obsession with buying the winery. Maybe he wanted to force Ethan into a position to sell.

"He has access to the bottling room," Scott said. "Do you think he could have messed with those bottles?"

"We saw him coming out of Megan's room. He was as confused as we were."

"He doesn't seem like much of an actor," Scott admitted.

Treasure squirmed in her arms. "I saw him at the Cluster. What if he did something to the wine they served that night?" Aury's anger was rising just thinking about what Ethan was going through. "Do you think Megan's in on it too?"

She put the puppy down, and Scott took her hand as they walked toward the main building. "We can't be sure there's an 'it' to be in on. We need to talk to them first."

Treasure followed close on their heels. *Maybe she's picking up on Elvis's protective nature,* Aury thought.

The sun hovered low above the hills when they entered the tasting room through the open sliding glass doors from the porch. Megan had returned, red-eyed but no longer crying. Matthew had pulled a mini-wine cooler from under the bar and was conducting a deep clean behind it. Wine glasses and coasters were lined up in a perfect row across the bar top like soldiers. Even the displaced cooler rested flush against the bar. Matthew looked up when they entered.

He answered their unspoken question. "We've been meaning to get to this for a while, but there's never been the time. Thought I'd go ahead and knock it out."

Treasure stuck her nose into the small space. Matthew pushed her away gently.

Cleaning? Aury eyed him curiously. She approached Megan, who was replacing glasses on the overhead racks. "Are you doing all right?"

Megan sniffled. "I went to school with Kevin. He was quiet but a nice guy. We went out a few times."

Matthew glanced up at the comment, then bent his head and increased his scrubbing efforts.

"Ethan isn't capable of hurting someone like this," Megan went on. "But if it wasn't him . . ." she trailed off.

"Who do you think it is?" Aury pressed.

Megan gazed at her earnestly. "People think I'm crazy, but I'm not. They don't see the things I see."

"What did you see?" Aury gently stroked her arm, like calming a skittish horse.

With a deep breath, Megan reeled off her theory. "I see lights all the time, bobbing through the fields late at night. It isn't Ethan. I asked him. Sometimes if I'm outside too close to sunset, I hear noises. Creepy, like something crawling out of a grave. I've even heard the eerie wails of the Seneca warrior." She shivered. "The furniture in here didn't move itself, and I sure didn't do it. It stopped when I did the cleansing. Then there were the nails in the parking lot, and the wine bottles exploding. This place is haunted. That's all there is to it."

Aury waited to see if there was more. When Megan averted her eyes, Aury took her hands. "There must be a logical explanation. I don't think the Seneca warrior has a beef with the Songscape Winery or Ethan. And your cleansing worked; you said so yourself. I think some of these things must be of human origin."

Treasure put her front paws on Aury's legs looking for attention. When Aury ignored her, Treasure wandered off.

"My grandma said this place has a bad aura. She didn't want me to work here."

"Are you and your grandmother close? Liza is my grandmother and my best friend." She shot Scott a loving smile. "My best *girl*friend."

Megan relaxed as she spoke kindly. "Grandma taught me everything I know about crystals and cleansings. She's famous around here when folks want their lands and houses blessed."

"Maybe you can help us get to the bottom of all this strangeness." Aury's soothing voice quieted Megan's jumpiness.

Scott leaned his elbows on the bar near where Matthew was cleaning. "Aury saw you at Flo's during the party."

Matthew didn't meet Scott's eyes. "So?"

"You didn't stick around. Don't you like to paint?"

The young man stood and dropped the scrub brush into the bucket of water. "I wasn't there for the party." He dried his hands on a towel.

"Why were you there?" Aury asked.

"I had to drop the wine for Ethan."

"The party had already started. Wine was flowing." Scott kept his voice conversational.

Matthew shrugged. "Flo knew she under-ordered and asked me to bring more."

"Ethan didn't mention a second delivery," Scott said.

"She called the winery, and I answered. Ethan was already gone. I knew he wouldn't mind and would bill her later. With everything going on, I didn't get around to writing it up."

"Why were you talking to Chantel?"

At this, Megan dropped Aury's hands and crossed her arms. She stared at Matthew intently.

"We were just talking. I'm allowed to talk to people."

"I saw her give you something." Aury addressed Matthew but kept one eye on Megan's reactions.

He stiffened. Reluctantly, he answered, "She was tipping me for helping her out."

"Helping her how?" Scott didn't sound friendly anymore.

Matthew glared at him. "None of your business."

"Like poisoning wine?" Scott persisted.

"Kevin died," Megan squeaked out.

Matthew's face softened as he gazed at her. "Megan, it's not like that."

Scott stood straighter, towering over the man's much smaller frame.

Aury wanted to defuse the mounting tension. "Why don't you tell us what happened? We'll help explain it to Ethan."

"It was nothing." His words rushed out as if a dam had broken. "When I was delivering the wine to Flo, Chantel asked me to carry boxes in from her truck as well. I didn't see any harm in it. At the party, she slipped me a tip and made a joke about not telling Ethan I was working for the competition. I hadn't thought about it like that. We all help each other up here."

"What was Chantel doing at Cluster before the party?" Aury asked.

"She was putting the white wines on ice and arranging glasses when I saw her." Matthew nervously checked the tuck in his shirt.

Aury thought through scenarios. "Were the boxes in her truck from her winery?"

Matthew nodded. "It was her Riesling."

Scott looked at Aury. "I thought only Ethan's wines were served at the party."

"They were. Chantel made a big deal about being snubbed by her friend." Aury supposed Chantel could have brought a supply of her own wine earlier and that's how she was restocking her purse for their table. She could have been sharing her stash with other tables as well, undermining Flo's attempt to showcase Songscape Wines. "It could have been for another event Flo was planning." Aury thought of the withering vines. "Are you sure there wasn't anything else you were helping her with?"

Matthew's voice was sharp. "Like what?"

Had she struck a nerve? "Maybe having to do with the fake soil sample you provided to Mr. Reese?"

Matthew's face flushed, and Aury thought he might be sick. "You switched the samples, didn't you?"

He hung his head, tears forming in his eyes. "I was afraid it was my fault. The dying vines, I mean. I didn't do it on purpose."

"What did you do?" Scott straightened, hands clenched at his side. His anger simmered.

"I was trying to get rid of the critters. I didn't know it would hurt the vines. Chantel said it was safe for use around the plants. When the vines started to die, I was afraid I caused it. I didn't want Ethan to find out, so I switched out the soil samples. I stopped spraying as soon as I realized what was happening, but I'm afraid it was too late." Matthew wiped sweaty hands on his pants, leaving dark spots.

"You weren't doing it to ruin Ethan's vines?" Aury made her question as direct as possible.

"I wouldn't do that! I love this winery. I want to own it someday. I wouldn't do anything to hurt its reputation or its grapes." His eyes were pleading as he spoke to her.

Aury believed Matthew's story.

But that still left the question of what Chantel was up to at Flo's.

Chapter 15

Ethan resolved to keep Songscape closed for an extra day as he sorted through everything that had happened. He wanted to be alone while Joyce was at work, so Scott, Aury, and Liza decided to see more of the area. Ethan told them not to worry about the puppy, and they left Treasure snoozing in his dog bed. They drove to Watkins Glen, stopping at various roadside waterfalls along the way to take pictures. In the village, they strolled through the boutiques and antique stores.

After they finished eating lunch at Seneca Harbor Station on the lake, Liza pushed their plates aside and pulled out the tourist brochures she had been picking up along the way. She opened a few and handed one to Aury. "I know you two are itching to go hiking. Why don't you drop me at the Corning Museum of Glass? It'll take me a few hours to get through it. That will give you plenty of time to explore Watkins Glen State Park. Says here there are nineteen different waterfalls."

"We don't want to abandon you," Aury said.

"Ridiculous. This way I won't have you pestering me to read faster. I can take my time. I have my cell phone and will let you know when I'm about done."

Aury admired her grandmother's spirit. Although she was getting up in age, nothing slowed her down. She loved adventure and learning.

Thankfully she passed that on to me. Aury stood and

wrapped her arms around Gran's seated form. "You're the best, you know?"

Liza tapped her granddaughter's arms lovingly. "I think we're both pretty lucky."

After dropping Liza at the museum, Scott and Aury drove to the park. They made sure they had full water bottles before beginning the mile-and-a-half trail. They stopped often to take pictures, texting some to Liza when the signal allowed. Over two hours later, they returned to the car, hungry and ready for a glass of wine. Liza texted she was ready to go just as Scott pulled into the Corning Museum parking lot.

On the way back to Songscape, Liza filled them in on interesting facts she had picked up on her tour. They hardly got a word in, but Liza oohed and aahed over the pictures they sent her.

Dusk had fallen by the time they pulled up in front of the winery. Ethan and Joyce's cars were in front of their house, but the lights were low in the tasting room. The trio let themselves in and were greeted by a very excited puppy.

Aury bent down and picked her up. "We missed you too, Treasure. Have you been a good girl?"

Treasure licked her face with enthusiasm.

"Okay, okay. Let's get you outside."

"I'm going to lie down a spell," Liza said.

"I promised Ethan I'd double check his tests on the wine. I'll be in the cellar." He kissed Aury's cheek.

"It's just me and you, girl." Aury exited through the sliding glass doors to the patio and walked toward the lake. There was a slight nip in the air, but she wouldn't get cold as long as she didn't stay out long.

Treasure scurried ahead, looking back often to ensure her human was still following. Aury laughed as the puppy chased birds off the vines.

As they neared the lake, she spotted Megan and Matthew in deep conversation. Megan made grand gestures with her hands as she spoke, almost as if yelling, but her voice didn't reach Aury's ears. She averted her eyes so it wouldn't seem as if she was eavesdropping, but she sidled closer. Maybe they knew more than what they were admitting.

"That's ridiculous! Do you hear yourself?"

Aury had never heard Matthew speak in a nasty tone before. She was shocked it was the same finicky man who was always worried about the neat tuck of his shirts.

Megan matched his tone when she responded. "You are so one-dimensional! I should have known you couldn't open yourself up to other possibilities. Maybe I should talk to Ethan myself."

Treasure dove into a row of vines and started digging. Aury rushed to scold her. She scooped her up and repeated several times, "Leave it!"

A scream reverberated off the lake. Instinctively, Aury's head swiveled toward the young couple. Megan raced toward the main building, Matthew on her heels. He tripped, sprawling on the grass for a moment before pushing himself to his feet and limping after her. Aury held on to Treasure and followed them, but the wiggling puppy slowed her down.

Entering through the open barn doors at the base of the cellar, Aury called out for Scott.

"I'm in here. What's up?" He came out of the bottling room holding a clipboard with a pencil tucked behind his ear.

"I think Matthew may be trying to hurt Megan. I heard her scream." Aury was breathless as she set Treasure on the ground.

Scott put the clipboard on a stack of boxes. "Where are they?"

"They went into the tasting room."

Scott took the steps two at a time, bursting out of the doorway into the hall. Aury was right behind him.

Matthew stood outside Megan's door, pounding on it. His shirt was untucked, and his pants were covered in grass. "Megan, you're acting crazy. Let me in!"

"What's going on here?" Scott demanded.

Matthew's worried face turned to Scott. "I don't know. We

were talking by the lake, then all of a sudden, Megan screamed and ran. She locked herself in. She won't open the door."

Tears welled in his eyes, and he practically begged Megan through the door. "Megan, sweetheart, please tell me what's wrong. What scared you? Let's figure this out together."

Aury pushed Matthew aside and knocked gently on the door. "Megan, honey, it's Aury. Will you open the door for me? I want to make sure you're all right." When there was no answer, she spoke a little louder. "Scott and I are here. Nothing will happen to you. Will you talk to me?"

"We need to get a key from Ethan. It'll only take a few minutes." Scott gave Aury a questioning look.

She took in Matthew's despondent posture as he slumped against the wall. Realizing her split-second accusation of Matthew was probably premature, she nodded at Scott. "Go. You're faster. I'll be fine. Besides, Gran's upstairs if we need anything."

"Stay here." He raced out of the building.

Aury spoke to Matthew in a soft voice. "What were you arguing about by the lake?"

He looked at Aury quizzically. "What are you talking about?"

"I saw you fighting." She tried to keep the judgement out of her tone, going more for sympathetic. After all, all couples argue.

"You're spying on us? Did Ethan tell you to do that?" He stood straighter and pushed away from the wall. His worry over Megan switched to annoyance in an instant.

Aury was momentarily taken aback. *Was this the anger that sent Megan fleeing from him?* "It wasn't like that. I was taking Treasure for a walk. I couldn't help but overhear you."

"What did you hear?"

When she didn't answer right away, Matthew changed his tone. He must have sensed her wariness rising. "Listen, I'm sorry, okay? I'm a little stressed out right now. Things haven't exactly been going my way lately and now my girlfriend has locked herself in her room. I'm under a lot of pressure."

Ethan's running steps across the wooden floor stopped their conversation. He flew into the hall brandishing a ring of keys. Knocking firmly on her door, he called out, "Megan, it's Ethan. I'm coming in."

When he pushed the door open, Megan was lying on her bed on top of the covers, her hands clasped above her hips. She didn't move.

Matthew shoved past the others, reaching her side and sitting on the bed beside her. "Megan? Wake up. Didn't you hear us calling you?" He shook her shoulders, gently at first, then more forcefully.

Her eyes didn't open, but her hands came apart and fell to her side.

Matthew released an anguished cry. Ethan dialed 911 on his cell while Aury felt for a pulse. When none was found, Scott moved Megan to the floor and began CPR.

Aury held the weeping Matthew to keep him out of Scott's way. *It was so fast. She was just running across the lawn. Now this. How?*

Paramedics soon filled the small room and relieved Scott. Aury filled them in on what she knew and tried to estimate the time between events.

When Joyce burst in, Ethan wrapped his arms around her and led her back into the tasting room. Aury and Scott guided Matthew in the same direction. Liza stood by, wringing her hands, all signs of sleep gone from her eyes. The paramedics sped by with Megan strapped to a gurney, one attendant still performing CPR.

Before the sounds of their sirens had faded away, Sheriff Dines walked through the open door. "You're having an awful run of luck, Ethan."

"Not now, Sheriff. We need to get to the hospital."

"I heard the call on the radio. Two accidents in one week. Not very likely for this small town. I need to ask you some questions."

"We'll stay and answer them." Aury propelled Ethan and

Joyce toward the door. "I'm the one who saw Megan screaming and thought something might be wrong."

"I need to be with Megan," Matthew croaked.

"You should probably stay. The sheriff needs to know what happened by the lake." Scott took a hold of Matthew's scrawny bicep.

"We'll call you from the hospital," Ethan called over his shoulder.

Liza slipped into the kitchen while the others took a seat around a large table. Matthew buried his face in his arms and sobbed.

"Okay, Miss St. Clair. Let's start with you." Dines pulled out a notebook.

Aury conveyed what she saw, from seeing Matthew and Megan at the lake until they opened the door and found Megan lying in her bed.

Wordlessly, Liza returned, placing cups of coffee in front of everyone at the table. Gratefully, Aury wrapped her cold hands around its warmth.

Dines took the offered mug from Liza. "And where were you?"

"Napping upstairs. The pounding woke me up, but it took me a while to make myself presentable to come down. I waited in this room. I didn't go down the hall. There were already plenty of people doing what they could."

The sheriff addressed Scott. "What were Ethan and Joyce doing when you got to their house?"

"Joyce was in the shower. Ethan was on the computer."

"And how long were you gone?"

He threw his hands up in the air. "It took me maybe three minutes to sprint to the house. Another two for Ethan to grab his keys and another three to sprint back. Ten minutes at the most."

"And what were you doing during this time?" Dines directed his question at Matthew.

"What do you think I was doing? I was begging Megan to open the door."

Aury nodded her agreement.

"When you opened the door, what did you see?" The sheriff stared intently at Aury.

"Megan was sleeping. At least that's how it looked. She was lying on the bed, hands folded. Peaceful." Aury shuddered. "But she didn't wake up. Even with all the racket we were making. I knew something was wrong."

Dines scribbled a few notes, but Aury couldn't read his chicken scratch. "Was anything in the room disturbed?"

She shook her head. "I didn't notice anything, but I wasn't looking at anything but Megan. I'm not sure I would be able to tell anyway. Matthew may be a better judge."

"Let's go take a look just in case, shall we? At least you can tell me what you touched." Dines stood. He pointed at Matthew. "You stay here for now."

Liza put an arm around his shoulders. "I'll stay with him."

Aury shot Matthew a sympathetic look. If the sheriff suspected he had anything to do with what happened to Megan, it wouldn't make sense to allow him back into the room.

Scott and Aury led the sheriff down the hallway. The bedspread was disheveled from when Scott had hastily moved Megan to the floor. Plastic wrappers left behind by the paramedics littered the carpet.

"Were the lights on or off?" Dines asked.

"The bedside light was on. Ethan turned on the overhead when he opened the door." Aury peered around at the neatly kept space. Childlike throw pillows shaped like cartoon characters were stacked in an easy chair next to the window. A few framed photos were lined up on her dresser. Books that Megan may never read were piled on her bedside stand next to a carved wooden box. On a tiny shelf hanging on the wall, seven crystals glittered in various hues. A faint scent of sage was overpowered by the antiseptic odor brought in with the first responders. Beyond the open bathroom door, sparkling fish stuck to the glass of the shower.

"Don't come in any farther and don't touch anything."

Dines stepped into the small bathroom. A half glass of water rested next to a toothbrush on the vanity counter.

Aury tried to see things through the sheriff's eyes as he came back into the bedroom, opening the sliding doors to the closet, where things seemed to be thrown in haphazardly. Clothes hung crookedly on hangers; some had fallen, covering the stacks of shoes jumbled on the floor. He regarded the neatness of the room and the disorganization of the closet, and Aury could almost hear his thoughts.

"Matthew stays here sometimes," she offered. "He seems like the type who would prefer things to be just so."

Dines raised his eyebrows at her, then nodded. "When you were outside, you heard Megan scream. Could Matthew have done something to her?"

Aury shook her head. "I didn't see him do anything, but I had turned away to chase our puppy."

Dines walked to the window, pushing the dream catcher aside to check that the lock was still engaged. Then he shepherded Aury and Scott out of the room, closing the door behind him. Back in the tasting room, he took the seat opposite Matthew. "I need to ask you some questions."

Aury and Scott stood nearby, not wanting to interfere.

Matthew sniffled. He pulled a handkerchief from his back pocket and wiped his nose.

"Why were you and Megan by the lake?"

"We went for a walk. It's been tough to get any alone time lately." He glanced at Aury.

"What were you fighting about?" Dines leaned forward in his seat.

Matthew picked at a string on his sleeve. "Same old thing."

"Which is?" the sheriff prompted.

"She wants to leave the Finger Lakes. Says there's too much bad energy here."

"But you don't want to, I take it?"

"No way. I'm establishing myself here. I want to be a vintner someday. This is a great place to learn." Matthew sat back heavily in his chair, dropping his hands to his lap.

"What made her scream?" Aury couldn't stop herself from asking.

Matthew glared at her as if she had betrayed a secret. "Who knows? It wasn't anything I said. She saw something by the lake and started screaming about the warrior. Then she bolted for her room."

"The warrior?" Dines looked confused.

Scott rubbed Aury's arms to take away the goosebumps. "Megan believes in legends, crystals, and all things supernatural. The other day, she told us about the Seneca warrior haunting the lake."

Chapter 16

1770 Hasanoanda

Hasanoanda sat uncomfortably on the seats provided by the White men inside their stuffy canvas tent. The sky outside was cloudless, and a slight breeze kept the heat away. Why these men insisted on conducting business inside this dingy covering was beyond him.

The clan mother had honored his family by selecting Hasanoanda to be the intermediary with these new traders from England. He was still learning their language and had to interject French words to fill in the holes in his vocabulary, but they were communicating well enough for their purposes.

Kaintwakon stood quietly at the tent opening, taking in the discussion. Hasanoanda knew his son was silent for now but would question him at length on their ride home. He was an inquisitive one, always thirsting for knowledge. Soon, he would be sitting in this disagreeable chair, when enough time had passed for Hasanoanda to take his place as an elder.

The White man seated across from him held up a tool for Hasanoanda to inspect. He took it in both hands, turning the shiny object over carefully. The candlelight reflected off the metal.

"For cutting." The trader mimed sawing something on the table between them.

Hasanoanda touched the edge of the blade gently. A thin

slice of red appeared on his thumb. He was surprised, though he made certain not to show it on his face. The Nation had many knives made of obsidian and flint. He had seen shiny knives like these before when visiting other Haudenosaunee nations who had traded with the French, but none quite as sharp as these.

He set the blade back on the table. Silently, he signaled his son. Kaintwakon ducked out of the tent and quickly came back with one dark beaver pelt. He placed it on the table between the men.

The White man ran his hand through the fur, still soft and supple. "That will get you five."

"I can get ten from the French, not much farther up the river."

The Brit went through the act of considering it. Hasanoanda knew it was an act because he had seen it many times. The White men always underpriced what they were offered, so Hasanoanda had to exaggerate the value before they finally agreed to a trade that was acceptable.

This dance bored him.

"But it is farther. For eight, I will save you the trip."

Hasanoanda nodded his agreement.

"I have many more I can trade with you," the White man said.

"How many?"

"Because I see a long partnership in the future, I will give you forty-five like this for five pelts. That's more than a fair trade."

Hasanoanda considered a moment. Genessee would be pleased with a sharp tool like this. It would make skinning much easier and faster. But he didn't want to appear too eager. "Let us start with thirty for three furs. If they are as useful as you promise, I will see about getting more next time."

"Five pelts and I'll throw in three hand axes, a handful of awls, and a couple yards of wool for your wife to try. You won't be disappointed." The White man held his hand out.

The warrior was used to this custom but didn't care for

it. His word was enough. Adding the handshake did not make it any more binding. He shook the man's hand anyway. It seemed to make the Englishman happy.

Outside, the exchange was made. Hasanoanda had also bartered for articles of clothing for the winter and colorful beads for the Nation elders in exchange for their abundance of the Three Sisters. The latest harvest of squash, corn, and beans had filled the stores in the longhouses and left them enough to trade. Beaver furs were harder to come by. Once they had been plentiful, but the White man's greed had dwindled their numbers. Of course, it was the Haudenosaunee who were providing those pelts, so perhaps they were showing signs of greed themselves.

Hasanoanda turned away at the smell of the noxious liquid the trader had offered him. It had been a good day. He wouldn't ruin it by clouding his mind with the trader's drink.

As expected, as soon as they were outside the White man's camp, Kaintwakon started with the questions. "What are the knives made from?"

"Steel, so I am told."

"Will they stay sharp forever?"

"Surely they will lose their edge after a time. I think we will be able to make it sharp again. We will need to experiment."

"I'm glad you got the awls. It makes punching through leather so much easier. Mother will be pleased."

Hasanoanda nodded. He was pleased with the trade. The more he learned of the British and French, the easier it was to anticipate their needs. They still struggled with farming because they insisted on planting items they were used to in their home countries but which were not as viable in this land.

"Did you taste the drink he offered? I could smell it from where I stood beside the horses, and that's saying something." Kaintwakon swatted at a deer fly that landed on his leg.

Hasanoanda answered his son's questions the best he could, then they transitioned to practicing new English words. He made a mental list of words he needed to learn during their next meeting.

"Why don't the French and the English trade with each other?" his son asked.

"I'm sure some of them do when needed. But for now, the traders' home countries across the ocean do not get along, so these men don't get along." Hasanoanda had struggled with the concept at first as well. Now he accepted it and tried to use it to his advantage.

Chapter 17

Present day

The dark circles under Ethan's eyes were prominent when he stumbled into the tasting room the next morning. He joined Aury, Scott, and Liza at a wooden table as they finished their late breakfast. "Joyce and I stayed at the hospital until Megan was pronounced dead. Then we had to meet up with Sheriff Dines at the station early this morning to answer his questions and provide information about Megan's next of kin. Joyce had an important meeting to go to, then she'll be home early. We didn't get much sleep." As if to emphasize this, he yawned.

Aury's heart ached that she hadn't been able to get to the bottom of Ethan's troubles yet. First Kevin, now Megan. She was having trouble making the connection. Matthew had turned a bit green when Megan mentioned she had known Kevin from school, but if jealousy was the problem, Kevin's death would have put an end to that. Why kill Megan?

"Is there anything we can do for you?" Scott asked.

Ethan ran his fingers across his scalp and rubbed the back of his head. His hair stood up in strange spikes, but he took no notice. "I can't imagine having to tell Megan's parents. No one should outlive their child."

There really wasn't a good response to that. Aury agreed wholeheartedly, but Megan's death had also covered Aury with waves of grief over her parents' loss, still too fresh to her.

"It's one thing after the other, isn't it? What was I thinking?" Ethan hung his head.

"This isn't your fault." Aury gave him a comforting hug.

He produced a weak smile, but she was certain he blamed himself for everything that transpired on his property.

"After such a late night, and considering everything that's happening, I'm not opening today. I'm sure Matthew is devastated." Ethan huffed out a deep breath.

Liza arrived on cue, placing a steaming cup of coffee in front of him. "Have you heard anything from the sheriff?"

Ethan sipped gratefully. "He took some things from Megan's room to be analyzed. At first glance, he doesn't suspect foul play. She didn't look like she was fighting anyone off. The door and window were locked, and the three of you stood outside. He doesn't see how anyone could have gotten in."

That left only one other option. "Is he thinking suicide?" Aury's voice was hushed. "What reason would she have to kill herself?"

"He sent a small, carved wooden box from her nightstand and the water glass by her sink to the lab. There may have been something inside the box that she took." He set his mug on the table. "I'm sorry you're stuck in the middle of all this. Why don't you get out of here for a while? There's more to the Finger Lakes besides murder, I promise. Check out some of the great waterfalls you haven't explored yet."

Scott and Aury exchanged worried looks.

"I'll be fine," Ethan assured them. "I want to check on Matthew, then I'm going to take a nap."

Liza took a seat across from Ethan. "I'll stay here. I want to organize my notes anyway. I've learned so many interesting things about this area."

Reassured there was nothing they could accomplish by staying at Songscape, Aury and Scott returned to their room to change into clothes more appropriate for hiking and tossed items into a backpack. Aury loved being outdoors, and although she was sad about Megan's passing, exploring might clear her mind so she could figure out what was going on and help Ethan and Joyce.

On their way through the tasting room, Aury kissed her grandmother's cheek. "We're taking Treasure with us. Call us if you learn anything new."

Scott whistled for the pup, and she scampered through the glass doors, sliding on oversized paws as she tried to come to a stop in front of him. Elvis strolled in casually behind her.

"Do you want us to take Elvis?" he asked.

"That would be great. I don't get as much time as I'd like to take him on long hikes. His leash is behind the counter." Ethan started to get up, but Scott motioned him to stay where he was.

Thirty minutes later, Aury, Scott, and the two dogs parked in front of the hardware store and walked a block to the dog-friendly coffee shop. While Aury read the large chalkboard displayed over the counter, the bell to the door chimed.

"How good to see you again. I heard what happened last night. It's just awful."

Aury turned at the sound of Chantel's voice. *How did she find out already?*

Chantel prattled on. "You must be frightened to death, being there with all the strange happenings. I don't see how anyone can stand being in such a depressing place."

Her tone set Aury's teeth on edge as she bit back a retort.

"We don't find it at all depressing. It's a wonderful place. Ethan and Joyce are doing a great job with Songscape." Scott sidestepped Chantel and approached the counter to place an order.

Aury noticed he didn't offer to get anything for Chantel.

"You simply must come by Château Christee for a tasting—my treat. The view is amazing, if I do say so myself. And, of course, the wines are award-winning. Why, I've won the local festival for the last two years, or is it three?" Chantel tapped her chin, her heavily painted eyelashes fluttering toward the ceiling.

Aury wasn't impressed by Chantel's fake memory loss. Chantel or one of her friends had mentioned Christee wines winning the gold at the festival at least a dozen times during Flo's event. Aury chose not to respond.

"Where are you off to this early? Things must be in chaos at Ethan's place." Chantel probed for details.

Aury scratched Treasure behind the ears, distracting her from sniffing around Chantel's three-inch heels. "We're going hiking at the Deckertown Falls."

"Oh, you must try Docet Falls near Spencer on your way back. It's gorge-ous, as they say here in the Finger Lakes, but it's treacherous. It might not be for southerners like you. Where exactly did you say you're from again?"

"Virginia." Aury doubted Chantel had ever been on a hike in her life. She was relieved when Scott returned with their drinks and a bag of food. "We really need to get going," she told Chantel.

"Don't forget Docet Falls! Then swing by and let me know what you think. The wine's on me," Chantel called after them.

"How did you put up with her all night at the Cluster?" Scott muttered when they had exited the coffee shop.

"Thankfully she flitted about the room quite a bit, so I didn't have to spend too much time with her. I hate to admit that Docet Falls is on my list of places to visit. Maybe we can stop on the way back?"

Scott leaned in to kiss her as they walked. "As long as it's award-winning, darling." He imitated Chantel's voice well.

"You know, as Chantel just proved, this town is really small. Maybe someone can tell us more about when Megan and Kevin dated," Aury said, feigning nonchalance.

Scott barked a laugh. "I knew we weren't really going hiking." He shook his head in acceptance. "Where do you want to start?"

"Kevin worked for a few businesses around town. Let's start with the barbershop."

They tied the dogs to the red, white, and blue helix pole out front and pushed the door open. The jingle of the bell was drowned out by the many voices engaged in discussion. When an old barber noticed them, he called out for them to take a seat.

Aury picked a discarded newspaper from a plastic chair and placed it on top a stack of cascading magazines on an end table. She and Scott sat, but when he started to ask a question, she hushed him. "I want to hear what they're talking about."

He rolled his eyes, but kept his mouth closed.

The small space was full with four barbers all working diligently on customers, while a few bystanders leaned against countertops engaged in the conversations.

"But I *told* that boy," the old barber who had spoken to them said, "to keep his distance. He didn't need to get his mind twisted with her crazy notions."

The man in his chair jumped to the defense of the girl with the notions. "She isn't—wasn't—that bad. She was fed too much mumbo-jumbo by her grandma, that's all."

The men at the next station broke into cheers over something that happened on the television, drowning out the older barber's response.

"But that was years ago."

Aury only caught the tail end of the customer's reply. She strained to catch up with the conversation.

"And look what's happened now! Two young people dead. It's a shame, that's all. A darn shame." The barber whipped the white drape off the client with a flourish.

The man produced a few bills from his wallet and handed them to the barber. "See you at the funeral."

The barber pocketed the money and motioned for Scott to take his place. In the background, men continued to laugh and yell at the television screen.

Scott gave Aury a questioning look. "I just got a haircut before we left home," he whispered but stood anyway.

She patted his hand. "A little trim won't hurt. Try to get him talking."

Scott took his seat and allowed the barber to fasten the drape around his neck.

"I'm Harold. What brings you in today?" Harold addressed Scott's reflection.

Scott cleared his throat. "A little trim?"

The uncertainty in his voice didn't fool Harold. "Looks to me like you just had a trim. What do you really want?"

Aury gave up waiting on the sideline and approached the barber chair. "We were the ones who found Megan and are hoping to learn a little more about her. We didn't know her well."

Scott spun around in the chair to face them.

Harold eyed them. Aury felt him taking their measure, trying to decide what to tell them.

"Megan told me she used to date Kevin." Aury figured that was close enough to the truth. She had said they went out a few times. "How serious were they?"

"Umph." Harold dropped the scissors he was holding into a jar of blue liquid by the mirror. "That girl was never serious about anything. She led that poor boy on, making him think she was interested. Then she read his Tarot cards and told him it was over. She didn't see anything for them in her future. Just like that, she was on to the next boy, then the next."

Aury was surprised. Granted, she didn't know Megan well, but she seemed like a quiet, capable young lady. *How many other men did she lead on and dump? Could any of them want to hurt her?*

"Kevin wasn't as quick to get over her. He had such a kind heart and still held a torch for her. Even the day before he died, I think he was making plans to see her." Harold picked up the broom and swept around his area.

"What makes you think they were going to meet?" Scott asked.

"He was finishing up when I got here to open the shop. When I asked him why he was running late, he grinned like a schoolboy. Said he had something special planned. When I asked who the special someone was, he just shook his head and smiled bigger. He knew better than to talk to me about her. She broke his heart so many times over, I never wanted to hear her name."

Aury tried to remember what had been going on before the paint party. *Had Megan been working?*

While she wracked her brain, Scott kept Harold talking. "How do you know it was Megan? Maybe he met someone else."

"Another whacko into crystals and charms? Not likely." Harold filled, then emptied the dustpan. "Someone had left a bag on the counter. I didn't know who it belonged to, so I looked inside. As soon as I saw the sparkling gemstones, I knew. A few minutes later, Kevin rushed back in and grabbed up the bag. He ran out before I could talk to him about it. Doesn't matter. He probably knew what I'd say anyway."

His eyes turned sad. "Kevin was a fine man; just needed a little growing up, is all."

Aury placed a gentle hand on his arm. "We're sorry for his loss. We only bumped into him once, but folks we've talked to have nothing but nice things to say about him."

Harold nodded once, then his eyes grew hard. "But I can tell you this. Megan was certainly not the kind of girl who would do herself in. She was too full of herself for that."

The bell above the door sounded the arrival of another customer.

Scott stood and pulled apart the Velcro holding the drape around his neck. "Thanks for your time. We'll let you get back to work."

Harold held his hand out to Scott. "You're still getting charged for taking up my chair."

Chapter 18

After ferreting out what little dirt they could in town, Aury and Scott stood by their car, trying to decide what to do next. No one had given them anything more than what Harold knew. Some didn't even know that much.

"What about Kevin's mother?" Scott suggested.

Aury shuddered at the thought. "I don't want to drench up any old wounds for a grieving mother. I can't imagine what she's going through."

"All we know is that Megan and Kevin went out a few times. Only Harold has said anything about Kevin still holding a torch for her."

"And you think that's something he'd share with his mother? She sounds like the overprotective type. I don't think she would have approved. If she did think something was up, she probably would have pointed it out to the sheriff right away." Aury drummed her fingers on the roof of the car as she thought. "No, let's not talk to his mother. We should ask Ethan and Joyce though."

They put the dogs in the backseat and climbed into the car. "The dogs didn't get much exercise walking around town. Maybe we should go for a short hike. Docet Falls are really close."

As if Elvis understood, he leaned his head into the front seat and licked Scott's face.

Pushing him back and turning on the engine, he said, "At least that's decided."

A short drive later, they pulled into a nearly empty parking lot. Aury was surprised not to see more students taking advantage of the weather, then she remembered it was fall break. Maybe many of them had left town while they could.

"I hope Docet Trail lives up to the hype." Aury clicked the leash on the wiggling Treasure when they climbed out of the car.

Scott let Elvis out of the car. The older dog waited patiently for Scott to clip on the leash. Looking past Aury, Scott raised his arm in a wave.

Aury turned to look but saw only trees. "Who'd you see?"

He looked puzzled. "No one, I guess. I thought it was Matthew, but I could be wrong."

Treasure was excited for the hike. She pulled at the leash Aury had clipped to her collar, ready to explore the new smells and animals. Aury practiced a few "heel" commands, then let the dog sniff along the trail.

Initially they walked along in silence. Aury's thoughts bounced between Flo's party, Megan's death, and Matthew.

"Do you think Matthew was really just delivering more wine to the Cluster?" Aury pulled Treasure back from a patch of poison ivy.

Scott was used to Aury's mind palace and was able to join her train of thought easily. "He could have been. I mean, that's what he does for Ethan."

"But wouldn't Ethan know?"

"If he wasn't in the office when the call came in, it's not beyond reason that Megan or Matthew would have taken the order and fulfilled it. That's what he pays them for. Ethan can't be everywhere at once."

"But Ethan checked the records when the sheriff asked for them. He didn't mention an additional order."

Scott shrugged. "Matthew said he was in a hurry and hadn't filled out the paperwork yet. He planned on doing it the next morning, but then everything went off the rails."

"Still sounds fishy to me." She stopped on the trail and stared into the running water that ran alongside it, lost in her thoughts.

Elvis flopped onto the cool dirt, resting. His fluffy, white fur instantly attracted the brown particles. Aury made a mental note to brush him before they got into the car. "Why would Megan have something deadly in her room? She didn't seem to be mentally unwell or the type to consider suicide."

"We didn't know her really. Besides, the sheriff didn't say it was suicide. It could have been an accidental overdose."

"She appeared so peaceful when we found her. That was a sharp contrast after seeing her run screaming from Matthew. Do you believe his story about their fight?"

Scott started walking again. In the woods, more trees had begun to shed their leaves, and the shooshing of the leaves underfoot was almost as loud as the river along the path. "Does it matter? Do you think he had time to get into her room, kill her, and get out before we showed up?"

"No, I suppose not. But he did have access to the things in her room. He could have poisoned her earlier." Aury was starting to feel the effects of the uphill trek. There weren't many hills where they lived, let alone areas high enough for waterfalls.

"But what reason would he have?" Scott picked up a handful of pebbles, then tossed them one at a time. Treasure yipped and ran as close to the water as his leash would allow. Aury gave her a gentle tug to remind her of where she should be walking.

"I'm not sure. I wonder how well he knew Kevin. Did you see a spark of jealousy when Megan mentioned that she had gone out with him?"

"I didn't pick up on it, but that doesn't mean anything. It's a small town. They're bound to know each other."

She tried to come up with scenarios where Kevin and Matthew might have crossed paths. On a delivery? At a bar?

They were about the same age. Where did twenty-somethings hang out around here if it wasn't a winery?

"Aury? Are you still in there?" Scott tried to knock on her head when she stopped walking.

She shoved him playfully. Treasure wanted in on the game and jumped on him. Elvis plopped down again and watched them from his resting spot, not bothering to raise his head.

"Do you think there's more to Chantel and Matthew than they're saying?" A thought still tugged at Aury, but she couldn't narrow it down.

"She's a little old for him, don't you think?" He let Treasure pounce again, then easily rolled her over to rub her belly.

Aury made a face at him. "Not what I was getting at. I just don't buy that she was tipping him for carrying in some cases. Maybe they were up to something, and Megan found out."

"And that's why Matthew and Megan were fighting?" Scott didn't sound convinced.

"Chantel's involved somehow; I know it. You should have heard her at the paint party. Her cutting comments were mostly directed at Ethan and Songscape. I think she's threatened by him." Aury pulled a hairband from her pocket and expertly twisted her hair into a messy bun to get the strands out of her face.

"Possibly. But Ethan isn't her only competition. There are hundreds of wineries in the area." Scott observed Treasure's movements. She had given up on her attack on Scott and now circled Elvis. Her leash ruffled the leaves as it dragged across the ground, discrediting her sneaky approach.

"What if she has done similar things to discredit the other wineries?"

"Like poison their wines? I think someone would have noticed the trend."

"Not that extreme. But you said so yourself, Chantel spreads rumors. What if she poisoned the well with her words?"

Scott laughed. "I see what you did there. Cute." He followed Elvis as the dog got up and sniffed around the riverbank. "Okay, if you think Chantel is behind the two deaths, what's our next step?"

"I think we should stop by her winery on the way home and see what else we can find out about her." Aury slipped off her shoes and socks to walk into the cold pool at the base of the fall. As she braced her hand on the rock, Treasure spotted a butterfly. She jerked on the leash, tugging Aury off balance. When she tried to stop herself from falling, the leash fell from her hand. Treasure took advantage of the free rein to chase her newest friend.

"Treasure!" Aury called.

Elvis tugged at his leash. Scott took the hint and released him. "Go get her, boy."

Aury started to climb out of the water.

"I'll get them. You can wait here. I'm sure Elvis will herd Treasure back this way." Scott followed Elvis.

Aury tried to relax and enjoy the silence, but it was too quiet. The sound of Scott and the dogs traipsing through the woods had faded. She walked through the shallow pool, still warmed by the sun, despite the trees nearby. Her mind raced with theories and possible conspiracies to explain the two unusual deaths in such a short time. She glanced at her watch. It had been ten minutes. "Scott?"

When no answer came, she stepped out of the water and shuffled her feet on the grass beside the trail. Her feet were only semi-dry when she stuffed them back in her shoes. She rushed down the path Scott had taken. A five-minute walk brought her to the base of a cliff. The rumble of the twenty-foot waterfall explained why Scott couldn't hear anything. She laughed, watching Scott try to corner Treasure, who thought this was a wonderful game of tag. Elvis worked with Scott, nipping at Treasure to drive her toward the human.

A flash of color drew Aury's eye to the top of the cliff above Scott. As she stared, a large boulder shifted, rocked, and tipped over the edge. Aury screamed Scott's name.

Although he couldn't hear her, Elvis did. His ears perked up. He turned to Aury, then seemed to follow her line of sight to the danger. Barking, Elvis gave up on Treasure and dove at Scott. Thinking this was part of the game, Treasure joined in.

Scott fell back as the larger dog hit his chest. Treasure pounced seconds later with a yelp. Aury reached them moments after the rock hit the ground where Scott had been standing. Smaller stones and debris rolled down the hill, kicking dust into the air. She wrapped her arms around Scott's neck, tears streaming down her face. After ensuring Scott was fine, she turned to Elvis.

"What a good boy!" She scratched his ears and spoke directly to the Aussie. "You are my hero."

Scott sat up and took Treasure in his arms. She let out a sharp bark that transitioned into a whine. "Ah, Aury."

Aury continued to pet Elvis but looked at Scott.

He held up a hand, red with blood.

Aury's heart skipped a beat. "Are you okay?"

"It's not mine. It's Treasure's."

Chapter 19

Hours later, they emerged from the veterinary hospital. Treasure had a new bald spot and a few stitches where the vet had closed the inch-long cut on her hind quarters. Elvis stayed protectively by the pup's side when they approached Chateau Christee.

Scott and Aury selected a table on the open veranda overlooking the archways that led to a large, covered area shrouded in leafy vines. Aury wondered if the vines were real or ornamentation that would last throughout the year. The outdoor bars near the pavilion were closed up tight but stood ready to go when a party broke out—just add alcohol.

Aury pictured people dressed in ballgowns, twirling to orchestral music under twinkling lights. It was the perfect setting for a wedding. She almost laughed aloud when she realized where her mind had wandered.

Almost as soon as they settled, the click of heels on tile announced Chantel's arrival.

"I'm so glad you made it." Her words didn't match her expression, but it had been a long day, and Aury could have been imagining things.

Chantel must have spotted Scott's dusty clothes and blood smeared on Aury's t-shirt from holding Treasure in the car. "What happened? You look horrible!"

"Just a little problem on the trail. Nothing major.

Everyone's fine." Scott's quick dismissal signaled to Aury that he didn't want to share their adventures.

They had disagreed about whether or not to call the police about the incident at the falls. Scott argued there wasn't anything to report because Aury didn't actually see a person. He didn't want to potentially bring more attention to Ethan and Songscape. Aury didn't think Scott was taking the accident serious enough. Eventually they settled on calling the park ranger. At the very least, the area above needed to be checked for any other lose rocks that might fall.

"We thought we'd take you up on that tasting." Aury flashed a bright smile as Chantel visibly struggled to pull her eyes away from the stains on Aury's clothes.

Chantel cleared her throat. "Of course, let me get that started for you." She clicked away faster than she had arrived.

Scott laughed. "Do you think she's worried we'll get her chairs dirty?"

"She seemed more surprised than worried. Do you think she could have had anything to do with the rockslide?"

"How could she? You saw how she's dressed. No way she's been out hiking with all that makeup." He snorted. "Besides, those heels would get caught in the rocks."

Aury wasn't convinced. Something was still off about Chantel, and Aury didn't think it was solely that she disliked the woman. "If you don't think she has anything to do with it, is there a reason you didn't want to mention our mishap?"

"Chantel's a gossip. We don't need her spreading rumors about us that may affect Ethan." Scott lifted Treasure into his lap. She was still a little woozy from the medication.

"Based on our appearance, she'll be telling people we slaughtered someone at Songscape."

Scott grimaced. "At least we'll know she's the source of that rumor."

A young woman put two wine flights on wooden handles in front of them. She scurried off without a word and returned carrying a charcuterie board with bread, meats, and cheeses.

"Thanks, but we didn't order all this." Scott smiled, trying to lessen the girl's nervousness.

"It's okay. It's on the house. Let me know if there's anything else you may need." She practically curtsied before she hurried away.

Aury raised an eyebrow at Scott. "Is your charm scaring people away?"

He stroked Treasure gently. "Maybe she doesn't like dogs."

Elvis rested his head in Aury's lap. "Who can resist this face?" She scratched vigorously behind his ears, once again admiring his multicolored fur. It reminded her of a scrap quilt that came together so beautifully it seemed deliberate.

With a big sigh, she picked up the first glass with a two-ounce pour. Aury read the label beside it. "Chardonnay. Buttery with a note of vanilla."

Scott clicked her glass and sipped. "Not bad. I think it's sharper than Ethan's, but I'd have to taste them side by side."

"I wonder if Chantel has ever done that with Songscape's wines. She was pretty specific in her comments when she was slamming Ethan's wine."

"I wouldn't think it would be unusual to sample the competition."

They gazed out over the vineyard. It was a beautiful location with grapevines reaching the lake's edge. Some were newer vines, not yet showing signs of producing fruit, while others were obviously older, years into the production cycle.

Scott picked up the second glass. "This is the pinot grigio. Honeysuckle and green apple."

Aury closed her eyes, focusing on what she was supposed to taste. Sighing, she gave up. "I don't get it. It's good, but I don't taste apple."

Chantel pushed through the glass doors and made a beeline for their table. "I trust everything is marvelous here." She placed a hand on the back of Scott's chair as she surveyed the table.

"It's okay." Aury set her glass down and pushed it away.

Scott grinned at her snub and winked. "Since you're here, we were just talking about Matthew. He said he carried boxes of your wine into the Cluster the night of the party." Scott moved in his chair to lean away from Chantel's hand.

She hesitated before answering. "He brought in a few cases, yes. He's a nice young man."

"Why did you bring your wine to Flo's that night when you knew Songscape wines were being served?" Aury watched her closely. *Was Chantel blinking more than normal?*

"I knew some of my regulars would be there and might prefer my wine to anything else." Chantel sniffed. "Besides, Flo regularly stocks my wine for her gallery openings."

"Does the sheriff know your wines were served that night?" Scott turned up the heat.

She bristled at the question. "I only provided them for our table. I decided to let Ethan have his night."

"Does Matthew do work for you often?" Aury could tell the shift in subject rattled Chantel.

She sputtered a few times before answering. "What are you really asking?"

Aury decided the innocent charade didn't work for Chantel. She couldn't quite pull it off. "I'm asking if he's done other favors for you in the past."

"Like bringing you Songscape wine, for instance." Scott continued to pet Treasure, as if unconcerned with the answer.

Chantel gave him a measured look. "Why would I need wine from Songscape when I have the Christee quality?"

Aury made a mental note to check the invoices for any purchases delivered to Chantel. She thought about how to steer the conversation.

"How well do you know Matthew?" Scott to the rescue.

"Matthew has wanted to be a vintner since I've known him. He's always sniffing around, hoping to pick up some tricks of the trade, but he's simply too young. No one takes him seriously."

"Ethan values him," Aury said.

Chantel waved a dismissive hand. "Matthew has been

looking for a job at another winery for months. He'll certainly leave now that Megan's dead. I think she was the only reason he was hanging on there."

At the callous comment, Scott's head swiveled to look up at her, but he didn't respond.

"Speaking of leaving, how much longer will you be sticking around? You must be almost out of vacation days, right?" Chantel's friendly tone didn't soften her message.

"That's the beauty of owning our own business. We have unlimited sick days."

Aury's heart fluttered when Scott said "our" business. While he worked to turn Eastover into a Christian retreat center to fulfill his mother's dream, he had joyfully included Aury in all aspects of decision making and planning. They were partners in business and life, and they hadn't even set a wedding date yet.

"Besides," Scott went on, "with Megan gone, Ethan's going to need extra help. We'll probably stick around until everything settles down."

Chantel's face fell, but she recovered quickly. "With so much going on at Songscape, Ethan should cut his losses and drop out of the festival next weekend. He has so much to attend to."

"Oh, he'll pull it together. Don't worry about him." Aury didn't understand how people put up with this condescending woman.

"It's not just about him. We want the attendees to feel safe. We don't want a repeat of what happened at the party. Of course, I'm only saying this for the good of the community. Ethan and Joyce are new here. They wouldn't understand how much things like this festival mean to the livelihood of all the wineries on the Finger Lakes." Chantel stared pointedly at Scott. "His careless mistakes could have big repercussions on everyone."

Chapter 20

Aury stood behind the cash register at Songscape on the cushioned mat provided to save her from sore feet. Initially Ethan had been hesitant to reopen, but Friday night brought the perfect weather for the band hired to play on the back patio. With all the advertising done to promote the evening, Aury and Scott convinced Ethan to move ahead with their plans and reopen the tasting room. Nothing had pointed directly to Ethan's wine causing a problem, and Aury had faith that he would soon be exonerated.

While Scott and Aury poured glasses of wine and acted as cashiers, Ethan and Joyce focused on the tastings. A few of Ethan's part-time workers had pitched in to cover tonight. They ran food from the kitchen and washed glasses to keep up with the demand.

Aury was surprised when Matthew showed up to bus tables and seat guests. He was unusually quiet, even for him. Ethan hadn't been able to reach him the day before so was just as surprised when Matthew walked in, ready to work. Ethan tried to assure him it wasn't a problem to take time off to grieve, but the young man mumbled something about needing to be doing something. Ethan didn't press him. Aury tried to comfort Matthew, but he didn't want to talk about Megan.

More people showed up than Ethan expected. Sadly, Aury figured some came out of a morbid curiosity over Megan's death. She overheard more than one conversation about whether or not Megan's ghost would haunt the winery. Apparently, her belief in the supernatural was well known.

By the end of the night, Aury's feet were sore, in spite of the extra cushioning, but she felt the satisfaction of hard work and helping a friend. The band was packing up after their last set, and guests lingered over their wine, enjoying the cool night air next to the toasty firepits. Aury assisted Matthew with bussing the last tables on the patio. He still barely acknowledged her, but she couldn't blame him. She couldn't imagine what she would do if something happened to Scott.

Aury heard it first: the soft moaning intermixed with a sizzling noise. She quickly finished wiping the table and went to find Scott. When he finished bagging a customer's purchase, he gave Aury a quick kiss. "What's up?"

"Check the cameras. I think something's happening."

Ethan and Scott had spent the afternoon positioning wildlife cameras throughout Ethan's property. Determined to get to the bottom of whatever was going on with the spooky noises, Ethan had ordered the video cameras online a few days ago. They had been delivered that morning, and Scott had tied the feed to Ethan's computers.

Scott flipped open the laptop Ethan kept below the counter. Typing quickly, he brought up the live video feed. He clicked from one camera to the next.

"The noise was coming from the field near the lake." Aury strained her eyes to pick out details in the black and green images. "What's that?" She pointed to a dark shape. Nothing was that square in nature.

Scott zoomed the lens in for a closer view.

"What are you looking at?" Ethan came out of the kitchen, drying his hands on a towel.

"What's this in the field?" Aury pointed to the spot.

Ethan squinted at it. "Nothing I put out. It wasn't there when we set up the cameras. I think we would have noticed. I'll go check it out." Dropping the towel on the bar, he moved with purpose, graciously saying goodbye to customers he passed along the way.

Scott continued flipping through the feeds. Movement on one caught his eye. "Check this out."

On the screen, a tall, dark shape moved like a robot on an assembly line, repeating the same actions over and over.

"Where is that?" Aury leaned in closer to see.

"Where the vines were dying. Ethan wanted to figure out what animal has been tunneling out there."

"It's not a mole, but it *is* digging. Let's go see who it is." She found Joyce. "We're going to check something out. Be back in a minute."

Joyce waved at them distractedly as she continued ringing up the line of customers.

Aury grabbed Scott's hand and led him to the vineyard, trying to look as if they were going for a casual stroll, not to catch a criminal.

The digging motions didn't falter as they got closer. It wasn't until Scott shone a flashlight on the figure that he ceased his actions like a child caught in the candy jar.

"Care to explain yourself?" Scott asked.

Rodney gathered himself and stood tall. "I don't have to explain anything to you."

Scott cocked an eyebrow at him. "It's us or the sheriff."

The old man threw his shovel to the ground. "This here land belongs to the Reese family. It was given to my great-great-grandpap by the federal government as part of his Colonial Army retirement."

"Your father sold it legally. You don't have a claim." Ethan crossed his arms.

"He didn't know what he was selling. Tolar took advantage of him."

Aury watched the exchange, not wanting to ruin Scott's display of posturing. Reese appeared frail and ancient in the dim light of the lantern at his feet. It was hard to be intimidated by him.

"Why are you digging here?" Scott asked.

"None of your business."

"Do you really want to go that route?" Scott sounded exasperated.

After a brief hesitation, Reese responded in a whisper. "Treasure."

"What?" Scott and Aury exclaimed together.

The old man became excited in his manner, and his voice rose an octave as he produced paper from his back pocket. "The Haudenosaunee speak of treasure on this land. I don't know exactly where, but I've searched my property and haven't found nothing. That pup of yours was digging around here. Maybe she senses it."

Aury took the paper. It was a photocopy from an old journal dated September 26, 1779. She scanned it quickly. The British settler Geoffrey Lawrence befriended the Haudenosaunee and wrote of a conversation with a warrior. The Native Americans spoke highly of the riches of this land along the Seneca Lake, shared among the nations of the Haudenosaunee Confederacy.

She flipped the paper over. The writer referred to a vast fortune the Haudenosaunee were forced to leave behind when they were pushed further west—something they couldn't take with them.

"I figure it's gold. The natives traded with British soldiers. They had a taste of what White men were willing to pay." Reese's eyes glowed with greed.

Aury read the document more slowly. "It doesn't say anything about gold."

Reese sneered. "Of course not. Are you simple? They weren't about to give away their secrets. But no way did they come back for it. This land has been in my family since it was gifted to my ancestors as part of a land grant after we beat them British in the Revolutionary War. It has to be here."

"Wait, have you been sneaking around Songscape for months now?" A few things clicked into place for Aury.

"I wouldn't call it sneaking," Reese hedged. "I have been looking for treasure that rightly belongs to me."

"Were you on the lake Wednesday night?"

Reese had the decency to look shamefaced. "I was. The lake belongs to everyone."

"You were the warrior ghost Megan saw."

"I didn't mean to scare her. She took off before I had a chance to say anything to her. That dimwit followed her, so I figured she'd be fine."

"She's not fine. She's dead." Scott didn't try to soften the blow.

"I heard." Reese removed his hat and ran his fingers through his thin hair before replacing the cap. "Megan was a bit dotty in her beliefs, but she was a good kid. She's been to the house with my granddaughter quite a few times."

"When was the last time she was over?"

"Right before she did that cockamamie cleansing of the tasting room." Reese snorted. "To think she reckoned ghosts moved furniture."

"Do you know otherwise?"

"Just 'cause I know it weren't ghosts doesn't mean I know who did it," Reese snapped.

Aury gave him a reproachful look. He knew more than he was saying.

"I think it's time you moved on." Scott picked up the shovel and handed it to the old man. "Next time, we *will* call the sheriff. Like it or not, this isn't your land anymore."

Rodney snatched the tool and huffed away.

Aury and Scott watched him go. "If Reese was on the lake when Megan died, he couldn't have killed her," Scott said.

"But he said she's been to his house. He could have given her something. She may have taken poison, but we don't know if it was on purpose or by accident. It's suspicious that something scared her, then she ended up dead."

"I wonder if the sheriff found out anything more about the box on her nightstand." Shining the flashlight, he led the way back to the tasting room.

When they reached the patio, Ethan and Joyce were inspecting a large black speaker. "Meet our intruder. Someone left it out in the field." Ethan pushed a button. Strange moans, groans, and creeks emitted from the speaker.

"I think we know who." Scott filled them in on the encounter with Rodney.

"So he put this out to distract attention away from where he was digging?" Joyce crossed her arms, leaning back on the bar.

"He's not the brightest criminal. Any idea what treasure he's talking about?" Aury asked.

"I've never heard of a buried treasure around here. It's not like there were many pirates in the Finger Lakes." Ethan turned a chair around and sat on it backward.

Aury tapped her index finger against her chin. "Whatever it is, was it worth killing for—twice?"

Chapter 21

1775 Genessee

Genessee watched from the edge of the lake as the men rowed to shore. The boat was riding high in the water; that meant fishing was not good.

Hasanoanda smiled upon seeing her, but it didn't reach his eyes. The fish had been getting more and more scarce since the Europeans arrived. At first, the Haudenosaunee were happy to share and teach them about the fish in the waters. But, as always, the White man wanted more. Instead of only taking what was necessary, they over-fished, smoking and drying the fish in barrels to be shipped away from this land.

They had done the same with hunting. The warriors were traveling farther to find large game. The corn, beans, and squash their *moiety* planted still fared well. Between the eight clans, they were able to produce enough food to trade with the English. She had to admit, the farming tools Hasanoanda had received in exchange over the years had made the planting much easier.

The grapevines they received from the French flourished. In the French camps, instead of planting the vines and letting the Creator direct their growth, the farmers insisted on cutting them back every year and trying to control their yield. The Haudenosaunee vines produced more than enough fruit for the village as well as the birds, squirrels, and opossums.

Attracting the smaller creatures also created hunting grounds for the younger children to learn on.

The nuts from the hickory tree still provided sustenance for bread, but now the British were cutting down trees to build their homes. Things were changing, and Genessee didn't like it.

She also wasn't fond of the changes in her son or his friends. Understanding that the White men were here to stay, Genessee accepted the interaction necessary for trade. She didn't even balk when Kaintwakon began using English phrases, although her grandmother was not at all pleased.

When the fishermen had cleaned out the boat, Hasanoanda approached Genessee and pulled her from her thoughts. "How nice that you came to welcome me home." This time, his eyes did smile.

She swatted him lightly. "It's not as if I didn't just see you this morning. I only wanted to see you working."

He wrapped sweat-drenched arms around her and stole a kiss.

She pushed his chest. "Jump in that lake and rinse off before starting anything like that."

He kissed her again quickly and ran like a boy into the chilly waters of the lake, yelping and whooping as the other men jumped in too.

Heart fluttering, Genessee watched her husband of many years, remembering him as a young warrior. Their courtship had been very traditional and also inevitable. She always knew they would spend their old age together, and she relished the concept.

Worry crept over her face when her thoughts shifted to Kaintwakon. He hadn't shown much interest in the young ladies within their sister clans. Maybe when he and his father traveled with the hunting party, he would learn about other opportunities within the Nation. A little time away from his English friends would be good. She feared he was losing too much of himself in a rush to embrace the ways of the Europeans. Her brother still did his duty guiding Kaintwakon in the old ways. Her son could repeat the stories and knew the proper words for the Thanksgiving Address. He led the telling alongside his uncle before the last gathering. Through his words, Genessee knew her son did not take this world for granted, and for that, she was grateful.

Red and golden leaves fell around her. The men would be leaving soon. She couldn't guess how long they would be gone this time. They had to go so far, and that meant smoking the meat before they returned so it didn't spoil. She sighed. She missed her husband already.

As Hasanoanda emerged from the water, he sluiced the water from his caramel-brown, bare chest and muscular legs.

The sight of him still sent tingles through her body.

When he caught her eye, his grin was mischievous. He started toward her.

Genessee smiled back, then turned and ran for the longhouse.

Chapter 22

Present day

The sky was a brilliant blue with just enough fluffy clouds to make it look like a child's drawing. The slight breeze was a welcome as Aury and Scott tried to keep the table stocked at the festival and Liza collected money for the wine served. Ethan and Joyce chatted with the customers and served the wine.

Aury appreciated the ability to do *something* to help Ethan and Joyce, even if it was simply physical labor. Her mind continued to churn on the mystery surrounding the winery.

"Chantel wasn't exaggerating when she said this festival was huge. Everyone from the Finger Lakes must be here." Aury opened another case of wine, tucking the bottles into the ice to cool. The large metal tubs resembled feeding troughs for cattle.

"I'm glad we're here to help, but I admit I'm getting antsy to get back to Eastover." Scott collected empty bottles from the tables, replacing them in cases to be disposed of later. "I half-expected Matthew to be here, considering he said he wanted to work to keep his mind off things."

"Do you think he blames himself for Megan's death? He had access to her room. Or, if she did it to herself, was it over a fight they had? We only have his word that she claims to have seen a ghost." Aury took a piece of ice from the tub to wipe across her face, enjoying the momentary reprieve from the heat.

"Reese said he was on the lake and heard her scream. She probably saw him." Scott rearranged the full cases to make them easier to get to.

"But why would she kill herself over the warrior? She grew up with that story. It couldn't have been that scary." Megan seemed very young to Aury but not unstable. Her belief in ghosts, crystals, and cleansings was quirky, but Aury didn't think she would take her life. Could there be another reason she would willingly ingest poison?

Joyce called for a whole case of *Come Together* Catawba, pulling Aury from her musings.

"I feel bad for Matthew, but really, he could have at least let us know rather than leave us shorthanded. Ethan gave him the chance last night," Joyce muttered when Aury handed over the box. "Thank you for helping out."

Aury squeezed her shoulder reassuringly. "We're happy to be here."

Bells sounded over the loudspeaker across the fairgrounds. "That's the signal that the judging is about to start. Things will slow down here. Why don't you three check out the competition? You've been cooped up with us long enough." Joyce took the money box from Liza's table and stashed it under the counter.

"I could stretch my legs." Liza stood, hanging her handbag over her shoulder.

Scott looked at Aury and shrugged. "Let's see what all the excitement's about." He offered his arms to both ladies, and they strolled into the crowd.

The stream of people was headed toward brightly colored tents on the opposite end of the grounds from the vendor tables. Three women and two men, dressed in identical black polo shirts and khaki pants, talked quietly behind a table covered in a quilted cloth with a distinctly grape theme. Two wine bottles with labels covered were pulled from a special refrigerator and placed on the table. A steward opened the bottles and placed white wine glasses in front of the judges.

One judge poured a small amount into each glass. The other judges stepped forward and took a glass. Without speaking, each judge went through their own ritual of tasting the wine and jotting notes on their clipboards.

When they had all finished, the glasses were whisked away, replaced by red wine glasses with larger bowls. They repeated their pouring, tasting, and note taking, still not speaking. Aury didn't understand the excitement. Watching other people drink wine was boring.

Some others in the crowd must have had the same opinion, because slowly, people drifted away.

"Aury? Aury, is that you?"

She turned as Naomi approached, noting that the flashes of brilliant color in her flowing blouse gave her the look of a bird coming to roost.

"I told you that was her." Naomi directed the comment toward Ruthanne, who was hurrying to catch up.

Ruthanne was slightly winded when she reached them. "I'm glad to see you made it to the festival after all. Such a shame, all that's happening at Songscape."

Naomi's face reflected sympathy, but she didn't say anything.

Ruthanne fanned herself with an advertisement on a stick that had been handed out to people as they entered the festival. "Chantel said Ethan wasn't entering the competition this year. I really thought he had a chance too."

Scott's face lit up. "He entered a different wine. We helped pick it out."

Ruthanne appeared shocked, but Aury detected a small smile from Naomi.

"That's good to hear. We'll have to find a good seat for the results." Naomi's eyes sparkled with mischief.

"How does this work?" Liza asked. "The judges aren't saying anything."

"They don't want to influence each other's opinion during

the tasting portion. After they've tasted all the wines, they will confer, then make a decision." Ruthanne searched the crowd as she spoke.

"Who are you looking for?" Naomi asked.

Ruthanne's eyes darted to Aury and Scott. "I wonder if Chantel knows."

Naomi gently shook her friend's arm. "You are not her keeper. She'll figure it out when the results are announced."

The pasty woman rubbed her arm as if the light touch had wounded her. "I suppose."

"When you hear the bells sound again, the judges are ready to address the crowd. One of them will talk about each wine, describing its qualities. Usually they start with wines that don't make the cut, at least giving the vintners sound bites for advertising. Then they will uncover the label. Not even the judges know which wine is which until the label is revealed." Naomi waved her arms as if parting a curtain. "Then the top three whites and the top three reds are left. The judges will discuss each wine but won't show the labels until the end."

"They make it so dramatic." Ruthanne still glanced around, almost nervously.

"Are the judges from around here?" Scott asked.

"No. They come in from all over, but they're certified as sommeliers, meaning they're experts in everything wines, including food pairings," said Naomi.

"What do the winners get?" Liza asked.

When Naomi crossed her arms, her hands disappeared into the loose sleeves. "Bragging rights, really. This is all about marketing. People are going to drink what they like. That's all there is to it."

"Let's get something to eat before the results are read." Ruthanne tugged at Naomi's arm.

The woman let herself be pulled away, waving goodbye to the others.

"Not a bad idea. And I'd like to try some other wines." Scott led Aury and Liza to the food vendors.

After they had their fill, the trio circled back to the

Songscape tent to see how things were going. Foot traffic had picked up a bit, so they fell back into their work duties, keeping glasses full and collecting money. Joyce gave them a grateful smile.

When the bells chimed for the second time, it was like a moth to a flame. All the festival goers converged on the judges' tent. After ten minutes of waiting for the crowd to assemble and become somewhat attentive, one of the judges took up the microphone. She introduced herself and her team. She explained the rules and how the results would be announced. Naomi had been spot on.

"We'll begin with the red wine." The judge passed the microphone to her colleague, who read from prepared notes.

Aury tuned her out. Ethan hadn't entered a red wine this year. He wanted his best red to age another year before putting it in front of this kind of scrutiny. She surveyed the crowd. In the short time they had been in the Finger Lakes area, she could already pick out faces. Harold, the clerk from the hardware store, was chatting with Clara from the Grape Basket Quilt Shop. Aury couldn't hold back a grin when Clara placed a flirtatious hand on his shoulder and gave it a little shove.

The townspeople were having a great time on this beautiful afternoon. It was easy to forget poor Megan and the other troubles at Songscape. Hopefully Ethan and Joyce could forget about it for a few hours themselves.

When the announcer began discussing the white wines, Aury directed her concentration on what he was saying. She, Scott, and Liza clapped politely as the wines that had not won a medal were revealed.

Liza sighed. "I'm sorry to hear the wine from Lazy River didn't get in the finals. It's quite good. I had it with lunch."

"Like Naomi said, you like what you like. Let's get a few bottles before we leave." Scott gave Liza a one-armed hug.

When they were down to the last three white wines, Ethan's label had still not been exposed. Aury crossed her fingers. She wanted something to go right for Songscape.

The judge read his notes on the first wine. "A refreshing aroma of candied lemon and jasmine that doesn't disappoint with the taste of pineapple in a long finish."

He passed the microphone to the next judge, who read her notes on the second selection. "This full-bodied wine gives the strong aroma of apricots and honeycomb, but it surprises you with the intense grapefruit notes."

Aury elbowed Scott. "I thought Ethan pulled that wine."

"What wine?" Scott asked, a bit distracted by all the murmuring around them.

"*Jesus, Take the Wheel.* The wine served at Flo's party. He said he was pulling it because of the bad memories." Aury caught sight of Ethan near the judges' table. He was whispering something frantically to Joyce.

"What makes you think it's Ethan's wine the judge is describing?"

"Don't you remember? When we did our first wine tasting, Megan described the wine very much like that. Apricots and honey but tastes like grapefruit. It stuck with me because I didn't understand how grapes could take on the flavor of a different fruit."

Liza touched Aury's arm. "I read about that. It's a chemical reaction that just reminds you of a fruit you know. It's not really from cross-pollination or anything like that. Grapevines are self-pollinators."

"So what are the chances that another wine has the same chemical makeup of Ethan's—?"

"Shhh, I want to hear this next description." Scott took Aury's hand and kissed it.

The next judge's low voice carried through the loudspeakers. "With a subtle taste of lemongrass and nuts, this citrus-forward wine finishes very smooth."

Aury watched as Ethan nodded to something Joyce was saying to him.

A judge picked up a bottle, holding it high in the air. "For the bronze award, bottle number one. Princess Niagara from

Kingsville Cellars." The crowd clapped as he pulled off the paper covering the label.

Another judge held up a bottle, mocking the actions of the first. "For the silver award, *You May Be Right* Chardonnay of Songscape Winery."

Aury, Scott, and Liza clapped excitedly. Silver was wonderful for Ethan's first entry, but Aury still felt a little sad that he didn't take the gold.

When Chantel squealed, Aury didn't have to guess that the only remaining label must be from Chateau Christee. The judge confirmed the gold as Chantel's *Abeille* Riesling. Aury was going to have to get a bottle, if only to compare it to Ethan's Riesling.

Chapter 23

Sunday morning's overcast skies didn't dampen the festive mood at Songscape. Ethan and Joyce were overjoyed with the silver medal awarded to *You May Be Right*. After church, they insisted on celebrating by taking Aury, Scott, and Liza out for brunch at a nearby historic inn.

From the front, the gray-sided home was warm and welcoming. Harvest wreaths decorated every front-facing window, and a wrap-around porch held small tables where couples sat, taking their time over coffee and pastries. Aury's mouth watered when they passed the sweets on their way to their table.

When Aury caught sight of the view, she was glad Joyce had made reservations to ensure patio seating. It was strange seeing the lake from this angle. Aury didn't think she would have recognized it if she hadn't been told it was Seneca Lake.

Sitting on the deck, Ethan tried to point out where Songscape perched on a hill across the lake.

Aury had to tear her eyes off the scenery long enough to look over the menu.

During brunch, Joyce talked about her students. "I don't remember being that age. And thank goodness I didn't grow up with social media!"

They laughed at the memes Joyce shared with them, designed by clever Cornell students, that poked fun at various professors on campus. "Thankfully none of the jokes have been mean so far. While some of our faculty wouldn't know a meme if it was displayed in their classroom, others would be deeply hurt to think their students didn't revere them. Personally, I wouldn't put it past some of the younger professors to be adding their own memes to the mix."

When Aury couldn't eat another bite. She sat back and sipped a black coffee. "I certainly wouldn't get tired of these views."

"You need to see it in the winter. It's still beautiful, but the cold takes getting used to." Joyce waved to someone she knew at another table.

As a thought hit him, Ethan's face clouded over. "Megan loved the winter."

Joyce patted his hand. "She usually volunteered to open on snowy days, because she liked to see the winery surrounded in white powder, undisturbed before the shoveling began."

Ethan gave a tepid smile at the memory.

They sat in momentary silence. Aury was saddened at such a young life coming to an end before she had a chance to live. That got her thinking about Kevin. "I've been meaning to ask you, Ethan. Do you ever buy wine from other vineyards?"

He ruffled the hair on the back of his head and shook himself out of his funk. "To sell? No. To drink? Sure. I got into this business because I enjoy wine."

"Do you buy it by the case?"

"I've been known to on occasion, but it has to be really good and usually something they aren't likely to make again."

"Have you ever sold wine to Chantel?"

"Not personally. But she could have gotten it at the tasting room or a local store or restaurant."

"Even *Jesus, Take the Wheel*?" Aury persisted.

"No, we hadn't released that yet because I was saving it for the festival. I made an exception for Flo because she really wanted a Riesling."

"That's what I thought."

"What are you getting at?" Liza asked.

"Chantel was just so specific about Ethan's Riesling when

she was talking at the party. I figured she must have tasted it before, but I thought the Cluster was its debut."

Scott read her mind. "I wonder if someone slipped her a bottle or two."

"It doesn't really matter. She would have tasted it at the Cluster anyway." Joyce finished her coffee.

"I don't want to rush your lunch, but I need to get back." Ethan had taken advantage of the wine competition to advertise that he was hiring for positions in the tasting room. He had already lined up several interviews for the afternoon. With so many colleges in the area, a position like this was a great part-time job, especially for students on the hospitality track. "Please stay and enjoy as long as you want. There's also a charming trail down to the water that's a pleasant walk after eating."

Joyce stood with him. "After your walk, I recommend stopping back here for their Gewurztraminer. It's a refreshing white wine that hits the spot after a little exercise."

Ethan put his arm around her. "Joyce will come up with any excuse for a glass of wine. I think moving here may have been dangerous for her."

After the couple departed, Liza pulled a packet of sticky notes and a pen from her handbag. "Am I the only one who thinks it's strange that Matthew didn't make an appearance yesterday?"

Scott raised an eyebrow. "Are you always suspicious?"

"Yes," Aury and Liza said together. All three laughed.

Aury stared at her grandmother. "Do you think he was afraid of facing Ethan after conspiring with Chantel? That award-winning wine description sounded a lot like Ethan's *Jesus, Take the Wheel*."

"I'm sure he's still distraught after Megan's death. It's only been a few days." Scott took Aury's hand.

She ignored him.

Liza continued their line of thinking. "Matthew had his own motive for not wanting Ethan to succeed. He wanted to buy the winery and run it himself. He admitted to poisoning the vines and switching the soil sample. Is it possible he also thinks there's a treasure buried at Songscape?"

"Megan probably heard the stories when she was at Reese's house. That man raves like a lunatic. Maybe she told Matthew, and they cooked up a scheme to get the treasure for themselves." Aury's sentences came faster and faster.

Liza kept the pace. "What if Megan got cold feet and wanted to tell Ethan about the treasure? That could be what they were fighting about the night she died."

Aury's voice dropped to a stage whisper as she leaned forward in her seat. "He's in and out of her room all the time. He could have slipped something to Megan that she took without realizing it was poison."

Liza held up a finger. "Where does Chantel fit in?"

Aury thought about Chantel and Matthew's clandestine meeting at the Cluster. "Chantel told Matthew what to put on the vines that caused them to wither. Maybe she provided the poison for Megan too. Or Matthew could have been working with Chantel to make Ethan fail. She gets to keep all the awards, and Matthew buys the winery. Ethan trusts him, so might be willing to let it go at a better price to help him get started."

Liza played devil's advocate. "Matthew has access to the grounds anytime. If it was about the treasure, couldn't he just search for it whenever he wanted?"

Aury let this question tumble through her brain. "What if he did find it, but it's too big to get out without notice?"

Scott interrupted their conjuring with a burst of laughter. "Do you hear yourselves? What treasure? We don't even know if there is one."

"It's mentioned often in the books and journals I found at the local library. The writers don't say exactly what or where it is, just that it exists, and people have been searching for it for years. Maybe Mr. Reese has a piece of the puzzle we're missing." Liza scribbled something on her sticky notes.

"He has pages from the journal he showed us. Maybe there's more."

"You two are so sure Matthew has done wrong. What happened to the benefit of the doubt?" Scott crossed his arms, trying to look stern.

"The only way to know for sure is to confront him." Liza placed her notes and pen back in her bag.

Excitement radiated from Aury. "Just think, Scott, we may be able to find another treasure. This time it would benefit Ethan and Joyce. Can you imagine?"

They decided to forgo the walk to the water. Aury felt they were on the scent of something big, and she was anxious to get the answers. She and Liza continued to bounce ideas around while Scott tried to punch holes in their theories.

When they arrived at Songscape, Joyce and Ethan were sitting on the front porch of their house. Ethan had his head buried in his hands while Joyce gently rubbed his back.

Scott pulled into their driveway. "What's going on? I thought you had interviews to conduct?"

Ethan looked close to a breaking point. Aury wasn't sure what to say.

Joyce answered. "The sheriff called on our way home. They found Matthew's body at the base of Hector Falls. He's dead."

Chapter 24

1773 Kaintwakon

Birds called to one another as Kaintwakon stalked quietly through the forest. Ahead, the thick rack of a stag blended in with the branches around it. The young man lifted the bow to his cheek, took a deep breath, and pulled back on the string. His broad chest was bare, and his hair was tied back from his face.

He exhaled softly, preparing to release.

A twig snapped, and the stag swung his massive head toward the hunter.

Not wanting to miss his opportunity, Kaintwakon let the arrow fly, but it landed behind the retreating animal.

Kaintwakon turned to the teenager with pale skin and dirty blond hair. "Geoffrey, we talked about this. You cannot make so much noise." He shook his head. "Your skin glows so much, I'm surprised the stag didn't see you coming before he heard you."

"It was one small noise. You didn't even hear me before then." Geoffrey wiped the sweat from his brow with a dingy handkerchief, then stuffed it back in his pocket.

"At least you tried to camouflage this time."

Geoffrey's muscled chest was also bare, but he had coated it with mud, which was now dry and flaking off. "I do listen to some of your suggestions." He held up the pouch of herbs tied around his neck. "This really helped with the mosquitoes."

Kaintwakon moved forward in the trees, tracing the arrow's path. When he reached the area where the deer had been, he combed the ground carefully.

Geoffrey pushed bushes aside, helping with the search. "I'm sorry about the deer. Think we can find it again?"

"No, it's long gone. We can see if there's game closer to the creek if we hurry. The sun will be down soon."

Kaintwakon led the way. "I didn't expect to see you today."

"I have something to show you." He unslung the three-and-a-half foot long brown musket from his shoulder and held it out proudly.

"What is it?"

"It's called the Brown Bess. Father gave it to me for my eighteenth birthday." Geoffrey tried to load the musket as they walked but only succeeded in dropping paper packets onto the pine-covered forest floor. "Bloody hell!"

"But what do you use it for?" Kaintwakon stopped while Geoffrey picked them up.

"Let's just say you wouldn't have missed that stag if you had been using one of these."

"I wouldn't have missed the stag if you were quieter on your feet."

"I'll show you." Geoffrey held up one of the paper packets. "This is called a cartridge." He tore it open with his teeth.

He pushed back the hammer and opened the flash pan. After pouring a small amount of black powder from the cartridge onto the pan, he shut the frizzen to hold it in place. Holding the musket with the muzzle pointing up, he poured the rest of the powder into the barrel, followed by a lead ball.

Stuffing the paper into the barrel, Geoffrey rammed a steel rod into the barrel, packing it tightly into the breech.

"Let's go." Geoffrey took the lead.

As they neared the watering hole, the boys slowed their pace and silenced their steps. A large animal with dark fur drank from the rippling, crystal-clear water.

"What kind of creature is that?" Geoffrey mouthed.

143

Kaintwakon couldn't believe his eyes. The woodland caribou had not been seen in many seasons. Now, this majestic creature with a thick neck and enormous antlers stood within fifty yards. He raised his bow, but Geoffrey put a hand on his arm.

The Englishman raised the musket to his shoulder and sighted along the barrel. At the click that came with cocking the weapon, the massive caribou lifted its head. Geoffrey pulled the trigger.

The explosion split the air, and Kaintwakon dropped to his knees, covering his ears. He stared as Geoffrey raised his arm in triumph.

"I grazed it. Come on." He carried the musket in his left hand as he set off through the brush after the caribou.

They reached the edge of the river. Bright spots of red dotted the rocks, but the animal was gone. Kaintwakon tracked the trail of blood down the shore. When the trail ended, the warrior guessed the caribou had crossed the water. He waded in the rushing shallows, careful where he put his feet. Behind him, Geoffrey grunted as he wrestled to get his boots off before getting wet.

Kaintwakon pressed ahead. It wasn't good to leave a wounded animal.

He picked up the blood trail on the other side and followed it into the trees beyond. Sometimes he only spied droplets, while other areas were marked with large gushes of crimson. It couldn't be much farther now.

On a circle of grass under a weeping willow, the large beast was down on his side, huffing as he tried to breathe.

Tears stung Kaintwakon's eyes as he drew closer. The animal's hooves moved, as if he was trying to get to his feet, but he didn't have enough energy left.

The young man knelt, placing his hand on the caribou's flank. He sang a song to the Creator, thanking him for the bounty provided by this kill. He thanked the animal for his sacrifice and apologized for the pain caused by the poor shot. Pulling out his knife, he drew the steel blade across the animal's neck, cutting his lifeline and putting him out of his misery.

Kaintwakon's head was still bent low when Geoffrey jogged up behind him. "He's a beaut, isn't he?"

When the warrior turned to him, Geoffrey asked, "What's wrong? Are you hurt?"

"Keep that loud stick out of these woods! Do you not see the harm you've caused?"

Geoffrey's face screwed up in confusion. "You were going to kill him with your arrow. What's the difference?"

"Mine would have been a clean shot. The animal would not have suffered. The land gives us what we need. It is our duty to care for all the creatures and treat them with respect, even in death." Kaintwakon stood. He unwrapped a length of rope from around his waist and secured a knot around the animal's hind legs. He tossed the end of the rope over a high, thick tree branch.

Geoffrey caught it, and together they heaved until the caribou hung upside down, blood pooling underneath its head.

Chapter 25

Present day

They comforted Ethan the best they could but then left to give him time to grieve. Scott tackled the task of cancelling Ethan's appointments for the afternoon. Aury and Liza took Treasure and Elvis for a walk in the fields.

"There goes our theory about Matthew. I can't believe I was accusing him when he was lying at the bottom of the falls." Aury wiped away the tears pooling in her eyes and tossed a ball for Treasure to fetch. This made no sense to her.

"Not unless he felt so guilty that he jumped," Gran countered.

"I agree, it doesn't seem likely that it was an accident. Scott thought he saw him at Docet Falls. Living around here, maybe Matthew hikes regularly. A lot of locals do." She knelt and scratched Treasure's ears while she removed the wet ball from her mouth. Modeling this game with Elvis had made teaching it to Treasure much easier.

"Although Matthew didn't strike me as the jumping type."

Aury gave her grandmother a strange look. "What do you mean?"

Liza shook her head. "I mean *jumping*. Matthew was rather fastidious. The thought of leaving such a mess would have bothered him. If he were to kill himself, I think sleeping pills would be more his style."

Trying to step back and look at the problem logically helped Aury push aside the sadness churning inside her.

"That leaves Rodney Reese and Chantel Christee. I can't see either one of them climbing to the top of a waterfall." Aury tossed the ball for Elvis this time. While she held Treasure, she checked the puppy's stitches. The cut was healing well, no redness or swelling.

"Don't let looks deceive you. Reese has been working his land for years. He's probably in better shape than you think. If he thought Matthew was getting close to finding the treasure or even just buying the land, it might have given Reese a motive to kill him."

"Then do you think Reese is also the one who added something to the wine?" Aury picked up the slobber-covered ball and wiped it off in the grass before throwing it again, letting the dogs race to pick it up.

"You saw him near the bottling room when he didn't have a good reason to be there," Liza pointed out.

"I wonder if he had enough time to do any damage."

Liza adjusted her floppy hat, retying the colorful ribbon holding it in place. "I have a theory about that. I need to make another trip into town."

Aury waved to Scott as he walked out of the tasting room. "What's wrong now?"

Scott tapped his cell phone against his thigh. "Alan just called. His daughter fell and broke her leg. She'll be laid up a few weeks, and he needs to go help her out."

"That poor girl," Liza said.

"We need to get back to Eastover so he can leave. Sorry, Aury."

"But there's still so much we haven't figured out!"

"Alan said he can give us another few days to wrap up here. He's scheduling his flight out for Wednesday."

"We still don't know who tampered with Ethan's wines in the bottling room or at the Cluster." She encircled his waist with her arms. The notion of leaving this mystery unresolved didn't sit right with her. While she missed Eastover, Joyce and

Ethan were family, and they needed to clear their name and save the winery.

"We don't know that the bottles were tampered with. There were slightly elevated amounts of pressure in the bottles Ethan and I opened, which may mean the wine was still fermenting after the bottling process."

Liza's brow furrowed. "But I thought Ethan said he waited a few days after fermentation was done before he bottled those. How can it just start up again?"

"That's a good question for the experts. Ethan's consulting with Zachary from Cornell. He'll get to the bottom of it, so he doesn't make the same mistake again," Scott said.

"If he even made a mistake. It might have been Reese. What if he added yeast? Would that kickstart the fermentation process again?" Liza picked up the ball Treasure had lost interest in.

"Maybe. But that doesn't explain how it got into the bottles that were already corked." Aury was running with her grandmother's idea. "What about a needle and syringe? How big is yeast anyway?"

Liza pulled sticky pads from a pocket in her long skirt. She jotted down the questions to ask the vintner from Cornell. "What about the people who got sick at the Cluster?"

"With no bottles to test from the wine served during the party, we may never know what caused the problem. We've polished off quite a few bottles from that same batch and none of us got sick." Scott shrugged. "I don't know what else we can do."

"What's Ethan going to do without Megan and Matthew? How's he going to run this place?" Liza asked.

Scott regarded the vineyard. "He'll have to reschedule the interviews and try to get people to start right away. He has some part-time people already trained who can step up their hours until the positions are filled. Sure would make it easier to hire if he could explain Megan's death."

Aury and Joyce sat side by side on the Songscape patio as the sun set, listening to the insects call to one another.

"I feel horrible that I always seem to be working when Ethan needs me the most. I'm still establishing myself at the college, and as one of the few women on faculty in the engineering school, everything I do is scrutinized carefully. As much as I love my job, I hate the politics of it." Joyce sipped a glass of white wine. "Having you, Scott, and Liza here has lifted a burden from my shoulders. I'm sorry it isn't the vacation you were hoping for."

Aury touched her arm gently. "No need to be sorry. We're family, and we'll stick together."

Joyce sighed. "I'm worried about Ethan. This is hitting him hard. He got close to Megan and Matthew in a very short time. They had their quirks, but they were good kids. Ethan feels responsible."

"It's not like he could have done anything about their deaths. I mean, it wasn't as if something he did here was unsafe."

"That doesn't matter. Especially poor, sweet Megan. We didn't even notice she was so unhappy. What could we have done to make her feel more loved and accepted?" A small sob escaped Joyce's lips.

Aury put her arm around the woman. "She seemed happy enough to me." Aury thought about what Harold had said in reference to Megan flitting from man to man. Was she settling down with Matthew and getting more serious?

She decided not to bring it up. It didn't really matter now. "Listening to her describe the wine, you would have thought she was the vintner. She had a lot of pride in this place."

"So what do you think changed?"

Taking her time, Aury tried to sort out the pieces. "You know Matthew wanted to buy the winery, right?"

"Sure. He didn't hide that fact. He was pretty disappointed that the Tolars wouldn't sell to him directly, but he didn't take it out on us. He worked hard, but I think if a better opportunity presented itself, he'd be gone in a heartbeat. Matthew had his heart set on being a vintner."

"What was going on between him and Chantel?" Aury asked the question before she thought about the indelicacy of the matter.

If Joyce noticed Aury's discomfort, she didn't say. She wiped her eyes. "I think Chantel was trying to poach him from us. She often invited him to reserve wine tastings and coached him on wine making techniques. I didn't trust her though. She was a little too friendly. I couldn't help but wonder if she was using him to gain Songscape trade secrets—not that we have a lot. After all, Ethan's just learning. He asks more questions than he can answer, and most vintners are happy to give advice."

"So what's her deal?"

Another sigh. "All I know is hearsay." Joyce seemed to war within herself whether she should answer. Finally, she gave in. "Chantel plays the part of a sophisticate, but she was really born in Herkimer County, not too far from here. She lived in a tiny town and had few prospects."

"Really? Her accent doesn't sound like New York." Aury tried to pinpoint what Chantel's diction sounded like but couldn't.

"She's worked hard to change almost everything about herself. According to Clara and Mabel, Chantel met her husband in New York City. She'd gone to town with girlfriends, so they were all dolled up and playing a part. The poor man fell for it. 'Course he was twenty years her senior, so I'm sure that worked in her favor."

Aury leaned back in her seat. "Was he really French? The ladies were talking about it at the paint party."

"Probably somewhere in his distant past. His last name

was Christee, which I assume is French. But he was a New York who made money on Wall Street. The winery was probably just a place to invest and give him a weekend getaway."

"Does that mean Chantel did a lot with the winery? Is she actually the vintner or a figurehead?"

Joyce shrugged noncommittally. "I suspect Chantel is used to hard work. She grew up on a farm, one of many kids—five or six, I believe. When her husband died, a few skeletons fell out of the closet."

Aury's eye opened wide. "What kind of skeletons?"

"Apparently he didn't do as well in the stock market as Chantel thought. He had made some very risky investments that didn't pan out." Joyce sipped her wine slowly, drawing out the story. "Chantel never had children, and she didn't think her husband did either. She was quite surprised when a few extra people showed up at the reading of the will."

Aury gasped. She thought that kind of thing only happened in books.

Joyce continued, "Turned out, the will was ironclad with Chantel as the sole beneficiary. Didn't matter anyway; there wasn't much to inherit."

Aury sat quietly, soaking in the new information to see where it might play a part.

Eventually, Joyce finished her wine and stood. "But Chantel is a determined woman. She had to apply herself to keep the winery going or give up her charmed lifestyle."

Chapter 26

Monday morning, Liza positioned herself behind the bar in the tasting room. Aury loved that her grandmother took this responsibility so seriously. After a quick trip to the bookstore Sunday night, Liza had studied the wines and their descriptions. She even had Aury quiz her knowledge before breakfast that morning. Liza was ready to explain Songscape wines to any patrons who came in.

Scott and Ethan were tag-teaming the interview process to vet as many applicants as possible. Fall break was over, and Joyce was back at the college; that left Aury to do the grocery run into town. And maybe she could make a quick stop along the way.

The more she went over the unanswered questions from their visit, the more despondent she felt. Off to her right, Chateau Christee rested atop a hill. Aury turned into the long drive leading to the winery. No other cars were in the gravel lot, so she suspected the tasting room was probably closed on Mondays, like many others in the area. But she was there now. Maybe Chantel was around.

Aury approached the stone building warily, half expecting to see someone watching her from the turrets above. The lights inside were off, but the door to the tasting room was slightly ajar. She pushed it open quietly and entered the cool room. Chantel wasn't in the large, open space furnished with cloth-covered tables and high-backed chairs.

The last time Aury and Scott had stopped by, Aury's thoughts were occupied by their hiking incident at the falls and Treasure's injuries. Now she took her time to look around the room. The wall behind the bar which ran the length of the room was festooned with ribbons and awards for Chateau Christee's various wines. Aury had to admit Chantel had not exaggerated her success in the winemaking business. The awards dated back more than ten years.

Around the rest of the room, large framed photographs of various waterfalls in the Finger Lakes and in France decorated the walls. A small plaque next to each stated the location of the photograph and the photographer: Chantel Christee. Aury had to hand it to her. Chantel had an eye for capturing the falls at their best. Aury's favorite was a montage of Docet Falls from the same location in four different seasons.

In the gift shop, Aury found greeting cards that matched the photographs on the walls. In addition to the usual wine stoppers, charms, and painted glasses, beautifully carved wooden boxes adorned with grapes and vines held a collection of teas and herbs. Aury ran her fingers over the designs, suspicion growing inside her.

She completed her circuit, and no one had come out to greet her. Spotting a door behind the bar, she wondered if it led to the bottling area like at Songscape. The door was unlocked, so she went in, telling herself she was looking for Chantel.

Unlike at Ethan's, no steps led down to the winemaking area. Massive, stainless-steel vats loomed over Aury, making her feel like she had followed Alice's rabbit into a dream. Ethan had given such a good tour of his facilities, Aury was able to make out the various tools used for winemaking. She wandered through the building until she came to the racks holding hundreds of bottles of wine. Posterboard signs hung over certain sections of the racks, identifying which wines could be found there.

A portable label-making machine was set up next to the Riesling section. Aury read the *Abeille* label loaded in the machine. This was the wine that had won at the festival. Aury wanted to buy a bottle of it to compare to Ethan's. It struck her as curious that these bottles weren't already labeled if the wine was old enough to have been served at the festival. Maybe Chantel was going to add another award-winning stamp to the bottles.

Aury pulled a bottle from the rack to look at the label. No medal on it yet. As she replaced the bottle, she noticed a label stuck in the back of the rack that must have come loose. When she pulled it out, she was surprised that it was for Songscape's *Jesus, Take the Wheel* Riesling.

A door clicked shut behind her, and she spun around, tucking the label behind her back.

Chantel took her time crossing the bottling room floor to get to her.

Aury's mind reeled. "There you are. I've been looking everywhere for you." It was the best she could come up with on the spot.

"Everywhere indeed." Chantel appeared quite different in her Monday clothes. She still wore a full face of makeup, but her hair was pulled back in a ponytail, and she was much shorter in boots rather than her heels. She carried a camera with a telephoto lens, which she laid on a nearby workbench.

"The door to the tasting room was open. I waited there for a while, but when no one came out, I thought I'd see if you were in here."

"I see the closed sign didn't deter you. Did you find what you were looking for?"

"Well, I found you. We're heading back on Wednesday, and I wanted to get some of your gold medal wine from the festival." Aury strove to keep her tone upbeat and friendly.

"I can get that for you upstairs." Chantel eyed her suspiciously. "What's that behind your back?"

Aury tried to play it off. "Just trash I found on the floor." She crinkled it into a ball and stuck it in her pocket. "I was going to throw it away for you."

"I'll take it." Chantel held out her hand.

"No, it's okay."

"I insist." Her voice was as cold as the room.

Caught, Aury handed over the paper ball.

As Chantel opened the paper, a resolute look fell over her face. She sighed.

"I knew the description the judge gave of your wine sounded familiar. That's Ethan's wine." Aury added steel to her voice.

Chantel crossed her arms, eyeballing Aury. "You can't tell one wine from another. You as much as admitted that."

"I may not be able to pick out *floral notes* from wine, but that doesn't mean I can't pick out a cheat when I see one." Aury practically threw the words in her face.

"How dare you call me a cheat!"

She went on as if Chantel hadn't spoken. "What good does winning the award with Ethan's wine do you? You can't sell it." Then it hit her. She answered her own question. "No one tasted those bottles but the judges. They aren't from around here. Who would ever know the judges weren't tasting your wine? You slapped your label on Ethan's Riesling. Now you can put the gold medal on your wine, and no one will know the difference—except me."

Chantel's face went pale. "You are only guessing."

Aury indicated the bottles by the label machine. "Winemaking is a chemical reaction. If the judges tasted this wine, would it match your Riesling or Ethan's?"

The vintner's eyes shifted between Aury and the bottles.

"Was this your fallback plan because you couldn't get him to drop out of the competition after you tainted the wine at Flo's? Is a gold medal really worth killing someone over?"

"The wine at the Cluster was only supposed to make them sick. Your death will be more intentional." Chantel reached behind her back and pulled out a 9mm pistol. It was small, but at this range, Aury didn't doubt its ability to do the job.

She took a step back, furtively searching for a way out. "Do you always carry a weapon in your bottling room?"

Chantel snickered. "Lucky happenstance. I keep this on

me when I'm hiking in case I run into wildlife I don't want to meet up close. But no one would blame me for protecting myself against an intruder on a day I'm closed and clearly not expecting visitors. Or maybe the shot will be passed off as Land of the Lakes booming, and no one will even come looking for you."

Aury stalled as she tried to think of a way out of her situation. "We checked. There was no record of a sale to you or Chateau Christee for any Songscape wine. How did you get it? Matthew? That's what you were paying him for at the Cluster."

"Matthew was more than accommodating. He's been kissing up to me for years. He wanted me to sponsor him into this business. It didn't take much to have him deliver enough bottles here for me to tamper with. Then the fool actually carried them into the party for me without knowing it. They were in my wine cases."

"What did you do to the wine?" Aury moved closer to the wine rack and away from the gun.

Chantel waved the gun off-handedly. "A little diethylene glycol is all. It's not poison or anything. Not like antifreeze. Just makes the wine taste a little sweeter. It used to be a common practice."

"You mean until they discovered it was deadly."

"Only if taken in large amounts. How was I to know Kevin would drink so much?" Chantel shrugged, as if his death was of no importance to her.

"Where did he get his hands on it? He wasn't at the party."

"After I heard about Kevin's death, I took an inventory of my special bottles. There was one I didn't use because the cork was damaged. I found it empty in the garbage can. He must have downed the whole bottle. That was sad."

"What about Matthew? Did he know what you were up to?" In her curiosity, Aury's fear had almost vanished. Now she only wanted to get to the bottom of this mystery.

"That poor boy is so naïve. He had no idea until Kevin ended up dead. I told him he would be an accessory for getting me the wine." Chantel had the nerve to smirk.

Aury had never wanted to punch someone before, but the urge was growing strong in her. However, she needed the answers to her questions more.

"Why did he come after us on the trail? Or was that you? I didn't guess you were the nature type, but I was admiring your photographs upstairs. You're quite talented."

Chantel bowed her head at the compliment. "Everyone around here hikes. I have to keep my figure somehow. It's better exercise than the gym. But, no, I was working that day, if you remember. As it happens, Matthew was so distraught after poor Megan's death, he stopped by here. I told him about the wooden gift box you purchased from my shop when you first got to town."

"I didn't buy anything from you. I had never even been here until after the rockslide." Aury shook her head in disbelief.

"He didn't know that. He must have put two and two together and figured you got rid of Megan so you and Ethan's cousin could slip your way into replacing him and Megan at Songscape. After all, blood is thicker than water."

"That's ridiculous!" Aury's anger blotted out any remaining fear. "You gave Megan the poison in the box on her nightstand. What kind of tale did you spin to get her to take it willingly?"

"She was a jumpy little thing, always worried about spirits and hauntings. I shared a secret family recipe from my Native American ancestors to rid her of the ghosts. I don't often share that side of my lineage with people, so Megan was touched and promised to keep my secret. I knew she'd take it eventually, but I wasn't sure when. The timing worked out better than I could have planned."

"But why kill Megan? Did she find out what you were up to? Did she threaten to go to the police?" Aury took another half-step back and was stopped by the necks of the wine bottles jutting from the rack.

"Matthew told her about the wine delivery, and she stopped by to ask me about it. I couldn't take a chance she would rat me out. She traded her silence for a way to get rid of the ghosts once and for all. That and a promise to help Matthew get the winery." Chantel gave a short snort of laughter. "Instead of escaping them, she joined her ghost friends forever."

"You did all this for a wine competition?" Aury couldn't wrap her head around Chantel's disengagement from the consequences of her actions.

Her laugh was stronger this time. "No, darling. It's so much more than that. There's treasure on that property, and I'll be there to scoop up the deed when Ethan has to sell short to get out from under his failing winery."

"What do you know about the treasure?"

"I saw Rodney Reese's boney silhouette on the river on more than one occasion. That old goat talks a lot once he gets into his drink. When I confronted him about his slinking around late at night, he let it slip that he found an old treasure map. He just didn't know how to read it. At first I thought he was losing it, but then I talked to some history buffs who live around here. Seems Rodney might not be wrong. But I'll have plenty of time to search once the land is mine."

A puppy's yapping from outside the closed door snapped the invisible link between them. Chantel turned toward the sound, and Aury wrapped her fingers around the neck of a bottle in the wine rack behind her. Taking three quick steps forward, she swung the bottle with all her might, shattering the glass against the back of Chantel's head.

Chapter 27

The gun hit the ground and spun across the polished floor as the winery owner crumpled to the floor. Aury jumped over her body and kicked the gun under one of the racks. When she glanced back at Chantel, her dark hair had turned black with blood, and a shiny red pool was quickly growing around her.

"Aury? Are you in there?" Pounding on the locked door reminded Aury of the fortunate distraction that had saved her. Treasure continued to bark and scratch at the wood.

Shaking, she unlocked the door and fell into Scott's arms.

"Are you okay?" He held her close, returning the ferocity of her hug.

She stepped back and wiped her eyes.

When she turned to face Chantel, Scott got his first look at the body and the blood pool. Red footprints tracked from the body to the door.

He hugged her again. "Are you sure you're not hurt?" Treasure jumped on her legs, showing her concern.

"We need to call nine-one-one."

Scott led Aury to a nearby chair, and Treasure jumped into her lap. The puppy's wet tongue and cold nose did more good for Aury than a stiff drink would have.

Chantel moaned on the ground but didn't get up.

Scott placed the call to 911, then knelt beside Aury,

stroking her hair. "When you were gone so long, I knew something wasn't right."

"How did you find me?"

"Liza said you had narrowed down the poisoner to Rodney Reese or Chantel. I drove by Reese's first but didn't see your car. I was on my way to the store and realized that Chateau Christee was on the way. Thought I'd take a chance. What possessed you to come here on your own?"

Aury lowered her eyes. "I only stopped to buy a bottle of Chantel's Riesling. I wasn't doing any sleuthing."

"Until you did," Scott guessed.

She gave a weak smile. "The winery was closed, but the door was unlocked. I came looking for Chantel."

The distant sound of sirens grew closer.

"I wanted to compare her Riesling with Ethan's. The description the judges gave for her wine sounded too similar to Ethan's *Jesus, Take the Wheel*. That can't be a coincidence."

Scott touched his forehead to Aury's. "What am I going to do with you?"

While they waited for the ambulance, only Treasure's occasional whimper broke the silence.

The sheriff entered through the same door Scott had. "Why am I not surprised?" He stepped back out and signaled the all-clear for the medics.

While the gurney was wheeled in and the EMTs huddled over Chantel, Sheriff Dines quizzed Aury. "What brought you to Chateau Christee? Not enough wine for you at Songscape?"

She shook her head, trying to sort out all the details. "I thought about the comments I overheard at Flo's event about Ethan's wine being sweet. He said he didn't make sweet wines. I didn't think anything about it at the time because I don't understand the different distinctions very well. But after Ethan explained it to us, I would agree no one who knows anything about wines would describe his as more than semi-dry."

Dines considered her dumbly, clearly not making the connection.

"Ethan's wine wasn't served at the Cluster. At least not

as he intended it. Chantel admitted to adding something to the wine to make people sick. Dyethel-something. Whatever it was also made the wine taste sweeter. It must have killed Kevin." Aury grasped Scott's hand. "You need to tell Ethan, so he doesn't feel guilty."

She turned back to the sheriff. "Chantel told me she killed Megan too."

"It's your word against Chantel's. How can you prove it?" Sheriff Dines's eyes moved between Aury and Scott.

She pointed to the wall she had been backed against. "Well, for the wine, I bet if we test some of the bottles in that rack, we'll find Ethan's wine with a Christee label on it. That will prove she made the switch. If that's not enough for you, we can also get the judges from the festival to do a blind taste test. I'm sure they'll pick Ethan's out as the winner over Chantel's Riesling."

The medics rolled the gurney out the door, leaving a bloody trail with their wheels.

Aury shuddered. Treasure licked her face. "Yes, Treasure. I'm fine." She squeezed Scott's hand. "Thanks for coming to look for me."

Treasure jumped down and began sniffing around the wine racks.

"What about Megan?" Dines asked.

Aury filled him in on the rest of her conversation with Chantel.

"Doesn't explain how Chantel's head ended up a bloody mess." Dines crossed his arms and scowled.

When Treasure began to paw at the floor, Scott called to her. "Come here, girl. Leave that alone."

She barked twice, then stuck her nose under the shelf.

Dines raised an eyebrow but joined Treasure. Getting down on his knees, he removed his hat as he peered under the racks. Taking a pair of gloves from a pocket, he put them on and reached for the weapon. He held it up with two fingers. "Chantel's?"

Aury nodded. "She wasn't going to let me tell anyone about

the switch. That's probably why she couldn't resist bragging about tricking Megan into taking something poisonous."

They watched as Dines checked to ensure there wasn't a round in the chamber before bagging the gun.

"Sheriff, have you heard about a treasure being buried on Songscape? Chantel planned on ruining Ethan's business so she could buy up his land and look for it." Aury clapped her hands to call the puppy back to her side.

"There's always been speculation about a hidden treasure left behind when the six nations were pushed off this land. People have searched, but nothing's ever been found. Rodney Reese is a bit of a kook about it." He stroked his chin with two fingers. "If you want real answers, I suggest you visit the Seneca Arts and Cultural Center. They can give you a lot of information about the Haudenosaunee who live around here."

"Thanks, we'll do that." Scott held out a hand to help Aury to her feet.

"I need you to come by the station and make a statement. I think Ethan will be mighty grateful to put this mess to bed." Dines picked up his hat and walked with the couple to their cars.

Aury nodded toward the winery. "Before you go, you might want to have a look in the gift shop. You'll find a box identical to the one you found in Megan's room."

The sheriff allowed a small smile to break through his rough exterior. "I have some cold cases that are still unsolved if you are looking for more work, Miss St. Clair."

Chapter 28

1779 Kaintwakon

Dying and wounded filled what was left of the longhouses. Acrid smoke mingled with the metallic tinge of blood in the village.

Kaintwakon kneeled beside his mother, who held Hasanoanda's hand. The warrior was barely breathing. A hole in his stomach had been packed with cloth, trying to staunch the bleeding. It was soaked through.

"Where will we go?" Kaintwakon whispered so only his mother could hear. His heart hurt more than it ever had before. He hated seeing his father so weak and in pain.

Tears streamed down Genessee's cheeks. "We'll follow the herds. They've gone toward the setting sun. So must we."

"It's not fair." He knew he sounded like a petulant boy, but he couldn't help himself. His life had been turned upside down in a matter of days. Now they were going to leave the land that their ancestors had lived on for longer than anyone could remember. And for what? Because of the White man's greed?

She laid a hand on her son's head. "The Great Creator will direct our movements. We were here for a time. Now we will be somewhere else."

A scuffle at the edge of the camp drew their attention.

"Let me go. You know me." Geoffrey Lawrence's voice split the hush around the dying.

"Go to him," Genessee urged.

Kaintwakon darted the short distance, pushing aside his clan brothers. "He didn't do this. Let him pass."

Skeptically, the warriors let Geoffrey go.

"I came as soon as I heard." He gazed around the village at the death and destruction. "What can I do?"

"White people have done enough," a young warrior nearby spat.

"Let's get out of here." Kaintwakon took Geoffrey's arm and led him toward the lake.

They were silent as they walked past the longhouses and away from the clan gathering.

When they reached the water, Geoffrey turned to his friend. "You have to believe me. My dad said the Continental Army was going after Fort Detroit. He didn't know they planned to come after the Haudenosuanee." Geoffrey looked shamefaced.

Kaintwakon stared across the water. Smoke still hung in the air, but here, the breeze from the lake provided a respite from the stench of death in the village. "Where were your troops when the army came? Why didn't you stand with us?"

"We gathered who we could, but it wasn't enough. We have more troops coming down from Canada." Geoffrey pleaded in desperation for understanding.

"Your leaders didn't believe when our scouts reported a pending attack. You waited too long." Kaintwakon was exhausted.

"We'll rally. When our forces muster, we can take the Americans." Geoffrey tried to sound confident, but his demeanor gave him away.

"The army has already started their retreat, destroying villages as they go."

There was no good response to that dreadful truth.

"How's your dad?" Geoffrey scooped up a handful of rocks, tossing them in the air and catching them.

Kaintwakon knew he did this to keep his shaky hands busy. Geoffrey was never good at being still.

"Not good. I don't know if he'll be strong enough to travel."

Geoffrey fumbled his next catch and many of the stones hit the rocky beach. "Travel where? Where will you go?"

Kaintwakon's anger flared. "Does it matter? The White men want us gone."

"Not all White men. Come to the garrison. We can share the food we have."

"Your rations were often provided by the Haudenosuanee. They burned our fields and orchards. Where do you think you're going to get food to feed your troops? You cannot help us."

"Can't you stay here and rebuild? We can at least provide seed. I'll bring it myself."

Kaintwakon shook his head. "My people don't have enough meat to sustain us here. Now the land we used for farming has been destroyed. We would starve before we could plant and harvest again."

"It won't be the same without you here." Geoffrey almost whispered the words.

"How do you think we feel? We've lived on this land for many generations. Much longer than any White man. This land is sacred. We are being forced to leave a vast fortune given to us by the Great Creator."

"Why don't you take it with you?"

Kaintwakon smiled sadly at him. "All this time you have spent with us and still you don't understand. This fortune is not something to take. It isn't owned by one Nation or another. We share among all who live here."

"But won't you need it where you're going?" Geoffrey threw the last rock and wiped his hands on his britches.

"The Creator will provide what we need. This treasure belongs to the White men now. But until they learn balance, the treasure will be hidden from them."

Chapter 29

Present day

Aury, Scott, Liza, and Ethan were lounging in the tasting room on the overstuffed furniture. The winery didn't open until noon, but they were enjoying a chilled glass of Chardonnay on their last day in the Finger Lakes.

"I'm sorry we didn't get to the bottom of everything." Aury leaned against Scott on the couch. Uneasiness still played in her mind. She didn't like the idea of leaving a job half-done.

Ethan gave a half-laugh. "This has been a busy few weeks for you. Not at all what you expected for a vacation, I'm sure."

"Probably didn't help with selecting a wedding destination either." Liza grimaced.

Scott tapped Liza's knee. "Don't you start."

She playfully slapped his hand.

Aury twirled her glass. "I'm just sure Rodney Reese had something to do with the mess in the bottling room."

"But he didn't have access to the bottles." Ethan sipped his wine.

Liza set her wine aside, hardly touching it. "That's why I went to the local bookstore. Such a cute shop. I picked up a card for Alan's niece. They also had lovely artwork—"

"Gran. Your point?" Aury interrupted her.

"Sorry, dear. I got to thinking about the Seneca Drums."

"I thought that was caused by gas trapped in pockets of rock," Scott said.

"It was, but it's what made them stop that's more important—salt mining."

"Not following you."

"Mines mean mine shafts, which mean tunnels. I pulled the plans for old salt mines. Did you know one ran right under your property?" She handed Ethan a copy of an old map.

He searched it carefully, running his finger along the lake until he found where his property started. "I never would have guessed. It wasn't in the surveyor's plan when I bought the vineyard."

"It wasn't profitable. Most of the salt in this area comes from under Cayuga Lake. This shaft was supposed to have been filled in and sealed for safety. But what if it wasn't? What if his grandfather decided to keep the tunnel? Prohibition made alcoholic beverages illegal from 1920 to 1933. That couldn't have been good for the winemakers." Liza glowed with pride at her discovery.

"Having a place to stash wine for special customers would have been helpful if the law came knocking," Scott pointed out.

Aury's imagination was fueled by the Nancy Drew and Hardy Boy books she read with Gran when she was little. "Do you think there could be a hidden tunnel into Songscape? Reese grew up playing on his grandfather's land. An adventurous little boy is bound to find every hidey hole."

"It would explain how he got in to tamper with the wine after they had been bottled." Ethan caught the excitement from the others.

"We need to take a closer look in the basement." Aury jumped to her feet.

All five filed down the stairs into the cellar, Aury leading the way. They spread out, each taking a different wall. Even Elvis and Treasure sniffed around.

Just when they were about to give up, Treasure barked.

She ran to Aury and then back to the steps. The puppy knelt on her front legs, haunches high, and continued to bark at nothing.

Aury got down on her knees beside her. "Okay, girl, we're paying attention. Good girl." She patted Treasure while trying to see what the dog was excited about. There didn't seem to be anything remarkable about the foot of the stairs where Treasure was focused.

"Wait a minute." Ethan rushed over. "I never noticed that before."

Dropping to his knees, he ran his hand over a faint crack in the wall. It wasn't straight but ran roughly parallel to the ground at about thigh height. He pushed in various places until there was a quiet click.

Aury held her breath as Ethan pushed on the wall and the bottom three steps moved along with it, sliding into the wall and revealing a dark hole with steps leading down.

Chapter 30

"Grab that flashlight hanging by the fire hydrant on the wall." Ethan peered into the darkness.

Scott handed him the light and glanced over Ethan's shoulder. "I'm game if you are."

"You're going into that creepy tunnel willingly?" Aury was surprised.

"It's not a graveyard." He smiled, giving her a quick kiss.

"I'll wait here," Liza said. "My luck, I'd get down there and not be able to get back up."

Aury took Scott's hand. "Let's go."

Treasure scampered down the steps behind them, not willing to be left out of the excitement.

The beam of the flashlight bounced off wooden posts and planks holding the earth at bay. Aury pulled out her cellphone and turned on the flashlight function. It wasn't near as strong as Ethan's, but it made her feel better.

"I can see where they probably stacked barrels along the walls here. It really opens up." Ethan pointed with his light.

"Sure gets narrow fast though," Scott commented. "How far do you think that tunnel goes?"

"I'd bet all the way to Reese's property." Aury's heart raced while they thought about what to do next.

Ethan made up their minds for them. "We can't stop now."

They followed him down the dark tunnel in a single file. Aury noted it was just wide enough to roll a barrel on its side. She reached up to touch the boards above her head. She had never been claustrophobic but was rethinking her assessment now.

A muffled scuttling in the distance caused them to freeze.

"Probably rats," Ethan said.

"Great. Thanks for adding that to my list of fears." Aury tried to laugh it off.

Scott squeezed her hand.

Treasure wound her way through their legs and pushed past them. She let out a sharp bark and streaked off into the darkness.

"Treasure, get back here," Aury hissed.

"We'll get her. Don't worry." Ethan picked up the pace.

Aury's concern about the puppy made her forget her anxiety over the closed-in space.

They rushed toward Treasure's barking, now loud and insistent.

"What the—Get off me, you mutt!" A male voice intermingled with the puppy's sounds of alarm.

Ahead, the tunnel curved sharply to the left and opened into a large cavern. Ethan's flashlight caught Reese in the face.

The old man held his hands up to shield his eyes, momentarily distracted away from Treasure's attention.

"Why am I not surprised?" Aury crossed her arms.

He tried to regain some of his dignity. "What are you doing on my property?"

"Technically, I think we're *under* your property." Scott picked up Treasure to keep her away from Reese.

"How long have you known about this tunnel?" Ethan asked.

"I don't have to answer your questions. Get on out of here." Reese made a shooing motion as if they would just go away.

"What is this place?" Aury shone her light around to

reflect off the solid stone walls. It was much bigger than she originally thought.

"It could have been a speak-easy, a place where folks drank during prohibition. They were often built underground or in caves." Ethan flicked his light around as well.

"This would definitely qualify." Aury shivered. "It's really cold down here."

Scott touched the wall, then rubbed his fingers together. "Dry. That's good."

"It's mine, that's what it is! You git off my property before I call the sheriff." Reese was regaining his bluster.

"Consider me called."

They turned toward the sound of Dines's voice as he approached from the tunnel.

"Sheriff, what are you doing here?" Ethan aimed his flashlight at the lawman's feet.

"I stopped by to give you an update. Liza told me you were down here. I couldn't believe it, so I had to check it out myself." He addressed Reese. "Rodney, what have you been up to?"

The man seemed even older under the bobbing flashlight beams. His gaunt face was accented in harsh shadows. "This is my property, and I want you all gone."

Treasure growled low from the protection of Scott's arms.

"That's a good idea. Why don't you and I go up to your place and have a little chat?" Dines took Reese's elbow. "Lead the way."

Reese shook off his hand and started walking.

"You folks get back to Songscape. I'll be there shortly." Dines's tone left no room for discussion.

A door opened in the distance, letting in sunlight. Then it thudded close, causing a puff of air to blow by Aury's face.

"Shine your light over there." Scott pointed to another opening in the cave wall.

All three walked toward it, Treasure squirming to break free from Scott's grasp. He relented and placed her on the ground. She sniffed ahead but stayed within reach of the light.

The tunnel was narrow but larger than the path to Songscape. The ceiling sloped down so that the men were forced to crouch over as they walked.

Treasure zigzagged around Aury's feet. When she placed a hand on the wall to steady herself, it came away wet.

"Check this out."

She looked up at Ethan's words. Stone steps were set into the earth on either side of a dirt ramp.

"I'll bet this is where they rolled the barrels up to the dock to transport them by boat." At the top of the steps, Scott pushed on wooden doors that reminded Aury of her grandmother's old root cellar. The double doors were set into the ground at a thirty-degree angle, opening up and out.

A fresh breeze off the lake cleared away the musty smell of the tunnels. Treasure bounded up the steps.

Out in the sunlight, Ethan placed his hands on his hips and peered around. He pointed up the hill. "There's the tasting room." Turning to his right, he gestured to the orchard. "Reese's house is behind those trees."

Aury walked onto the rickety dock. "There's a flat-bottom boat tucked in these reeds."

Treasure snapped at a turtle as it slipped into the water.

"Figures Reese has been playing Seneca Warrior." Scott joined her on the dock and studied the hill toward Songscape.

"Did he really think an old legend was going to scare me away?" Ethan asked.

"It was enough to scare Megan. He knew her through his granddaughter. Maybe he hoped her rantings would be bad for your business." Aury took in the view across the lake. This close to the water, it felt like she was in a basin with green sides curving up around her.

"He was probably your ghost in the winery too. I'll bet he's the one who was moving the furniture in the tasting room around. He could have easily slipped in through the tunnels after you closed for the night." Scott bounced up and down on the dock, testing how solid it was.

"Megan probably told Reese you were putting in cameras because you didn't have faith in her cleansing. That's why he knew to stop." Aury carefully made her way back to solid ground.

"We better head back and see what the sheriff wanted." Ethan started down the steps.

Scott jumped from the dock and took Aury's hand. "We'll take the scenic route—above ground."

Chapter 31

Liza and Joyce were upstairs making coffee when the trio traipsed into the kitchen.

"I thought you'd be frantic when we were gone so long." Aury hugged her grandmother as if it had been weeks since they had seen each other rather than an hour.

"Oh, I was getting nervous but when the sheriff went after you, I figured everything was under control. Sit and tell me what you found." Liza handed them each a mug, and they settled down in the tasting room in the overstuffed furniture.

When they finished their tale, Joyce said, "I missed all the excitement."

"It was more exciting in the retelling." Ethan kissed her.

Sheriff Dines entered the tasting room and joined the group. As he took a seat, he seemed more relaxed than previous visits.

Liza jumped up to get him a cup of coffee.

"You said you came to give us an update. What did you find?" Ethan leaned forward.

"Kevin's autopsy report showed acute liver failure. That didn't make any sense, given that no one ever saw him drink alcohol of any kind. Growing up, his mother was always very careful about what he ate and drank because of his allergies." Dines perched on the edge of his chair, elbows resting on his knees.

Liza returned and handed him a mug.

He nodded his thanks. "After Chantel mentioned diethylene glycol to you, I had the coroner run a test looking specifically for DEG. She found trace amounts in the bloodstream and suspects that, because of Kevin's allergies, his body reacted violently to what he ingested."

"Harold told us Kevin was planning on seeing Megan the day before he died. Maybe she spurned him again, and he wanted to drown his sorrows." Aury tucked a loose strand of hair behind her ear. "Maybe that's why she was so upset when she heard about his death. She could have felt guilty for treating him badly."

"Can you tie the DEG to Chantel?" Scott asked.

"I checked over her online purchases. It's surprising how easy it is to buy. Chantel didn't use her business credit card, but I found a chemical company in her search history on her computer. They confirmed shipping DEG to her home address." Dines sipped his coffee.

Aury set her mug on the coffee table. "Well, that explains the poisoning and Kevin's death. What about Megan and Matthew?"

"You were right about the wooden box. Chantel has those made specially for her shop by a local artisan. I confirmed that the stamp on the bottom was his. We can't prove that Chantel gave Megan something deadly, but I think with enough time, she'll admit it to us on record. She already told you as much, Miss St. Clair."

"And Matthew?" Joyce whispered.

Dines sat back. "He was a different sort of young man, but in light of all this, I don't think he killed himself. I went to Hector Falls and inspected the edge again. I thought the ground was just dusted up by hikers sneaking close to look at the falls, but it could've been signs of a struggle. No way to tell for sure. Not like there's muddy shoe prints or anything. Lots of people hike there."

"Including Chantel. She has pictures of Hector Falls hanging in her tasting room. She probably knows the area well." Aury realized she had stereotyped Chantel based on her high heels and makeup. She wouldn't make that mistake again.

"Let's just say I don't think Chantel limited herself to poisoning. After she got patched up at the hospital, she was relocated to accommodations that are much less to her liking. She's already starting to talk, if for no other reason than to get someone to pay attention to her." Dines swallowed the rest of his coffee and stood up.

"What are you going to do about Reese?" Liza asked. "He's a troublesome old coot."

"I put the fear of God into him. I don't think he'll be bothering you anymore, but you may want to do something about that tunnel. I'm not sure how safe it is."

"I'll get someone out to inspect it this week. I don't want to take any chances." Ethan stood and shook the sheriff's hand.

After he left, the others thought over the new information.

"If Reese snuck into your bottling room, what could he have added to make the corks pop?" Aury asked Ethan.

"With all that's been going on, I forgot to tell you that I talked with Zachary. We went over my journals together, and he analyzed one of the bottles that didn't explode but was from the same batch. Nothing was added. It was the temperature."

"The temperature?"

"Zachary said that batch was exposed to extreme temperatures. The wine got too hot and expanded, forcing the corks to pop out."

"Wouldn't you have noticed if it was that hot in your bottling room?" Scott asked.

Ethan threw up his hands. "You would think so, but I didn't."

An idea tugged at Aury's brain. "Wait a minute. What if Reese slipped in after we all left for the paint party? He could have messed with the thermostat."

"But we would have noticed next time we opened the doors," Joyce said.

"Not if he snuck back in later that night and set it back to the correct temperature. The door to the cellar was locked, so we didn't check out the bottling room that night. Everything could have been back to normal by the morning. He had over sixteen hours to wreak havoc." The theory sounded very plausible to Aury.

Ethan's eyes lit up. "He could have been trying to ruin my wines and was probably just as surprised as we were that the bottles exploded."

Liza put her hands together. "I think that ties everything up."

"But what was the treasure Reese was going on about?" Scott asked.

Aury grinned slyly. "I don't think it's a treasure in the traditional sense. Reese got the idea from an old journal written in the 1770s. He made the same mistake so many White men made at that time."

When they stared at her expectantly, she laughed. Staring off into the distance, she tried to recall the exact wording in the journal. "Riches of the land shared among the Nations of the Haudenosaunee Confederacy. Something about a vast fortune the Haudenosaunee were forced to leave behind—something they couldn't take with them."

"The land." Liza breathed out wistfully.

"The land," Aury confirmed. "The Haudenosaunee Confederacy had lived here long before the Europeans showed up. Native Americans treasure Mother Earth much more respectfully than we do. Here they had the lake for fishing, fertile ground for farming, salt for preserving, and woods for hunting. The Finger Lakes region was their treasure."

"It wouldn't hurt to see if we can partner with the Seneca Arts and Cultural Center on some projects. Maybe they can teach us a thing or two about farming." Joyce wrapped her arms around Ethan.

Liza raised her mug. "That calls for a drink."

########

Songscape Wines

Love Me Tender by Elvis Presley: Catawba in an oak barrel. Baked apples and nutmeg.

You May Be Right by Billy Joel: Chardonnay with lemongrass and nuts. Oaked in neutral French barrels, so it's very smooth.

That's Life by Frank Sinatra: Blend of Riesling and Chardonnay. Subtle aromas of peach and apple, with the buttery flavor of a traditional Chardonnay.

If I Can Dream by Elvis Presley: Blend of Catawba and Cab Franc. Peppery with the taste of plum on the backend.

Look What You Made Me Do by Taylor Swift: Cab Franc. Medium bodied, fruit-forward. Aged in stainless steel.

Come Together by the Beatles: Catawba with a touch of Cab Franc. Fun and fruity. Makes great slushies.

Under Pressure by Queen: Sparkling, dry Riesling. Fresh, crisp grapefruit acidity, with notes of spice, pear, and green apple. Pair with soft cheeses or buttery seafood dishes.

Jesus, Take the Wheel by Carrie Underwood: Dry Riesling. Full-bodied wine with strong aroma of apricots and honeycomb but surprises with the intense grapefruit notes.

Here I Am (The One That You Love) by Air Supply: Semi-sweet Riesling. More peaches than apricot. Aged in stainless steel. Pair with Thai or Indian cuisine or something with a fruit sauce.

Satisfaction by The Rolling Stones: Chardonnay. Buttery, rich creamy. oak barrel. Subtle apple taste with cloves. Pairs with pasta and pesto, butter-based sauces

9 to 5 by Dolly Parton: Catawba. Mild berry, bright smooth finish. Has sparkle to it. Aged in stainless steel barrel. Pair with fresh melon or strawberry shortcake. Great for bbq.

Author's note

My eldest daughter went to school at Cornell, so I enjoyed visiting many wineries and waterfalls in the Finger Lakes. It was only natural that Seneca Lake became the backdrop for Ethan and Joyce's winery. Songscape Winery doesn't exist anywhere but in my imagination, although I clearly see the rolling hills covered with grapevines. I long to spend time in and around a winery, walking the fields and sipping wine for breakfast.

Docet Falls also does not exist. I don't want to give anyone the idea that there is a waterfall in the Finger Lakes that is unsafe due to falling rocks. Hector Falls does exist. It is a beautiful waterfall, only three and half miles from Watkins Glen. While, sadly, there are too many people who die in and around waterfalls, I don't know of any deaths at Hector Falls.

Although many cozies play on book themes, I wanted to do something different. My younger daughter is constantly trying to get me to pay closer attention to song lyrics, so I was inspired to bring music into my cozy. I grew up listening to Elvis Presley, therefore Elvis became the perfect name for the herder who kept Treasure in line.

All the people in this story are fictional. I researched historical happenings from this timeframe to give the proper context and realism, but my story does not point to a particular recorded event.

Haudenosaunee (hoe-dee-no-SHOW-nee) means "people who build a house." The name refers to a confederation or alliance among six Native American nations who are more commonly known as the Iroquois Confederacy. Each nation has its own identity. I highly encourage you to check out this website for more information from the Smithsonian Institute.

https://americanindian.si.edu/sites/1/files/pdf/education/HaudenosauneeGuide.pdf

I spent a wonderful weekend at the Ganondagan Indigenous Music and Arts Festival, immersing myself in the music and culture of the Seneca Nation. The people were eager to answer my questions and steer me in the right direction to keep me from misrepresenting anything or unintentionally insulting the Native Americans. I found the book *And Grandma Said* by Tom Porter (Sakokwenionkwas) very helpful with the finer points of Haudenosaunee traditions.

I want to give a special thank you to Corey Christman of Bravery Wines. Also a military veteran, he listened to my ramblings and helped me come up with a plausible scenario—even if unlikely—that would fit my story. And he makes darn good wines!

If you have enjoyed *Oaky With a Hint of Murder,* we would love a review on whatever platform you are most comfortable with.

https://books2read.com/OakyWithAHintofMurder

If you want to learn how Aury and Scott met, checkout *Eastover Treasures.*

Chapter 1

September 10, 1861

M ary's long skirts swished as she hurried into the dining area. *Where do I even begin?* she thought.

James had already transported some belongings, but he left her to sort out household items. How could she decide what was worth saving and what wasn't?

If she cleared too many objects, they would suspect items were hidden and go searching. She must be selective. Opening the drawer of the buffet, she withdrew a handful of items, then opened the next drawer, slamming them shut as she moved on. She repeated this process until she had a small pile.

Brushing the loose hair off her forehead, she turned to the next room. *I don't know why he has to leave now. We are supposed to be plowing a new garden.*

Outside the window, the reins clinked as James hitched the horse to the wagon. Swiftly, she shifted her attention to the parlor and took the painting from over the mantle. A lighter rectangle was left on the wallpaper where it had been. Muttering words her mother wouldn't approve of, Mary replaced the painting. She spun to take in the rest of the space.

Everything is a treasure to me! How can James not understand that?

Mary's frustration was clouding her concentration. She needed to take a minute. She stopped in the library, admiring their collection of books. Her father was a generous man and often sent treasures he found on his trips to Philadelphia. With the fighting between the north and south, no packages had come recently. She picked up the leather-bound volume he had given her when she and James moved to Virginia.

I need to get back to my writing. Father will expect to hear all the details about country life when we travel north next.

But when will that be?

Looking around, she took a mental inventory. A drop of sweat threatened her eyes, but she wiped it away with the back of her hand. Then she heard the thunder of the boys' feet across the wood floor. They skittered into the room.

"Momma, can Frederick and I go to the river to catch frogs?" nine-year-old Thomas asked.

She put on a brave face. "What are you going to do with them once you catch them?"

"We can eat them," Frederick offered.

Thomas punched his arm. "That's foul."

"No, it's not. It's living off the land. You eat what you can catch. Isn't that right, Ma?" Frederick was only ten, but already starting to talk like his father.

She smiled at the towheaded boys. "Let's save the eating until it's necessary."

"But if those secesh take our house, we may have to live in the woods. Pa said so," Thomas insisted.

"Where did you learn that kind of language, young man?"

"Noah," both boys said together.

Mary rolled her eyes. "I'll have a talk with your brother. You may go down to the river but take a basket and bring some berries with you when you come back."

The boys were out the door before she had a chance to say anything else.

"Sarah?" Mary called.

The fourteen-year-old entered the library, carrying her latest sampler. "Yes, Ma."

"Will you get some of the quilts from the upstairs closet and bring them down?"

"Yes, ma'am."

Mary replaced the book on the shelf and plucked out another one, placing it on the side table. Then another.

"Momma?" Sarah's voice cut through Mary's wild purge. "We aren't moving all those books, are we?"

"And why not? Books have value." Mary turned away from the shelf and took in the overflowing stacks she had subconsciously built.

Sighing, she began replacing some volumes. "Why don't you help me pick the best ten to save?"

Chapter 2

Present Day

The breeze picked up as Aury St. Clair sat on the back deck of the rustic motel checking the latest weather forecast on her phone. The hurricane had shifted again, this time moving up the east coast of Florida. There was a fifty-fifty chance the weather that accompanied a storm of that size would miss their slice of Virginia all together.

Aury held the cell phone loosely in her lap and prepared to say goodbye to the solitude she had with nature. The breeze rustled the bushes surrounding the pond, sending a ripple across the water. The frogs were especially loud. Maybe they sensed the impending storm.

The phone's buzz joined Mother Nature's song, and Aury picked it up again. The cell reception was so bad this far into the woods that she was usually bombarded with text messages that had been waiting to find her phone as soon as it could get a signal. From the porch, she at least had a bar or two.

She glanced through them, answering a few from the accounting firm she worked for. They seemed to disregard the fact that she was on vacation. She tucked it away again, rising from the picnic bench.

As Aury opened the door, she was immediately flooded with the cacophony of sounds emanating from the women jammed into the open floor plan of the activities room. The concrete walls did little to absorb the sound, bouncing it around the hall until only emphasized syllables and harsh laughter could be discerned.

Aury slid into place behind her sewing machine, which rested on a table butted against three others. The ladies continued their banter.

"Finished with your phone sex?" Debbie asked.

"I was. Don't know about him," Aury answered, just as straight-faced.

Debbie cackled. "Guys have a harder time faking it," she said, reloading her bobbin and snapping the door closed on the casing. Her soft, gray curls framed a round face that was always quick with a smile, but it was her brightly colored sweatshirts that Aury appreciated. They usually had a quick-witted line printed on them in bold colors. Today was no different: "I'm glad no one can hear what I'm thinking" was printed in neon pink.

Pat gave Aury a speculative look. "What's the weather?"

"The hurricane is scheduled to hit the east side of Florida. They still don't know if it will turn, but it's moving fast."

Debbie shook her head. "I could be a weatherman and do a better job than those bozos."

Pat ignored her. "Do we need to consider packing up sooner than planned?" A tall woman with a dry sense of humor, Pat's imposing nature hid her inner spunk. It had taken a while for Aury to figure her out. Thankfully, Pat saved her sharpest retorts for Debbie.

"No way," Linda said from the next table. "I paid for six days, and I'm going to use all six." The hum of her machine charged over the fabric in a practiced clip. "My husband would never let me get this much done at home. I'm taking advantage of the getaway."

Aury turned her gaze to the sunlight streaming through the windows. "Looks like another beautiful day."

"You just never know with these storm patterns," Suzanne commented from across the table. "Hurricanes are fickle." She stood from her machine and limped toward the ironing board.

Aury tried to focus on one of the many projects she brought with her for this quilting retreat. She had been looking forward to it for so long, but now the projects were overwhelming, and she had trouble concentrating.

"Sam said he thinks we should head back early in case they shut the ferry down," Carla added. "Taking the twenty-minute ferry will be a lot better than the extra hour it would take if we had to go up toward Richmond and back down the peninsula."

She didn't sound worried, though. At least twenty years older than Aury and six inches shorter, Carla was a sweet soul with a positive attitude. She'd find the bright spot in the toughest situation.

"If it comes down to it, we'll close up shop. Anyone can leave whenever they want if they're nervous." Aury had spent months planning this retreat. She would hate for the weather to mess it up.

She looked around the room at the fifteen heads bent over their sewing machines and projects in various stages. Aury knew she needed to get some work done. When she got home, there would be many other projects that drew her attention away from her quilting. She wanted to get her entry for the Mid-Atlantic Quilt Festival completed before the week-long retreat ended.

At thirty-eight years old, Aury was one of the youngest in the room. Reconnecting with her grandmother through her quilting had proven a useful hobby to distract her from the what-might-have-beens that kept her awake at night. After her parents had died in a car crash four years ago, she had been wracked with guilt. They had been on their way to visit her because she was upset after yet-another argument with her husband. They drove through the night instead of waiting until the next day. A drunk driver crossed the centerline and ended their lives upon impact.

Even with her grandmother's constant assurances that it wasn't her fault, Aury still felt responsible. And her husband gave her no emotional support. She had followed him to

Williamsburg when he was offered a job, more to be near her grandmother but also as a last chance to make their marriage work. It ended less than a year later.

Now her grandmother was her best friend, and she loved spending time with her. Liza St. Clair had taught her to sew when Aury was only eight years old. They had made clothes and quilts for dolls when Aury visited on vacations. It wasn't until visiting a quilt show that Aury began to value quilting as an art, not as a necessity.

Aury leaned down to search through her fabric bag as a pretense to hide her welled-up eyes from the ladies at her table. Thinking of her grandmother stuck in the rehab hospital broke her heart. Liza was spry for eighty-one and would take on most challenges. It would be unfair to be taken out by the flu. Aury had tried to find someone else to take over the retreat so she could stay and care for her, but the old lady insisted she go. She said Aury would do more good there than at her bedside.

... to be continued.

About the Author

Dawn Brotherton is an award-winning author, Air Force veteran, and avid crafter. When she isn't writing, she can be found in her sewing room, designing new creations with either fabric or paint.

When it comes to exceptional writing, she draws on her experience as a colonel retired from the US Air Force as well as a softball coach and Girl Scout leader. Her variety of interests has led to a variety of genres including mystery, romance, young adult fantasy, middle grade sports, picture books, and nonfiction.

Keep in touch with Dawn via the web:

Website:

https://www.dawnbrothertonauthor.com/

Facebook:

https://www.facebook.com/DawnBrothertonAuthor

Instagram:

https://www.instagram.com/dawnbrothertonauthor/

Bookbub:

https://www.bookbub.com/authors/dawn-brotherton

Other Books by Dawn Brotherton

Eastover Treasure Cozy Mysteries
Eastover Treasures
Oaky With a Hint of Murder

Jackie Austin Mysteries
The Obsession (also available on audio)
Wind the Clock
Truth Has No Agenda

Romance
Untimely Love

Children's Books
If I Look Like You
Scout and Her Friends Activity Book

Lady Tigers Series
Trish's Team (book 1)
Margie Makes a Difference (book 2)
Nicole's New Friend (book 3)
Avery Appreciates True Friendship (book 4, written by
Paige Ashley Brotherton)
Tammy Tries Baseball (book 5)

Nonfiction
Baseball/Softball Scorebook
The Road to Publishing

Contributing Author to Nonfiction
A-10s Over Kosovo
Sisters in Arms
Water from Wellspring